An Audience

with

Lama

An Audience

with

Lama

'bhilash

Kalam aur Syahi

Published by :
Kalam Aur Syahi
B-502, Tower Apartments, Near TV Tower,
New Delhi-110034
Email : abhilash@mail-me.com
Follow us on Facebook: https://www.facebook.com/#!/Audience.Lama

First published in 2012.
©Copyright 'bhilash, 2012

Typeset by :
Aaditya Designing Services in 10 point Adobe Garamond Pro

Printed and bound in India

ISBN : 978-93-5067-560-1

Price : ₹100.00

Preface

This is a work of fiction. Any resemblance to people and places living or dead is deeply regretted and is just a matter of coincidence. The situation and circumstances portrayed are solely for the purpose of storytelling and need not be mistaken as a provocation or a ground for discrimination. Reader's discretion is recommended. This is not a historical account but a work of fiction.

Monday, 8ᵗʰ August 2011

"We are witnessing remarkable non-violent struggles for freedom and democracy. I am a firm believer in non-violence and people power and these events have shown once again that determined non-violent action can indeed bring about positive change..."

Ladies and Gentlemen he has come forward in traditional red, yellow and orange colours. His spectacles are aggrandizing the graveness of this date. Moments from now he will share the much anticipated news. Reading from an off-white sheet of handmade paper he addressed the people one last time as their political leader.

"As early as the 1960s, I have repeatedly stressed that Tibetans need a leader, elected freely by the Tibetan people, to whom I can devolve power. Now, we have clearly reached the time to put this into effect..."

Television screens across the globe showed His Holiness the 14ᵗʰ Dalai Lama addressing a congress in the North-Indian hill town of Dharamasala. He requested the Tibetan parliament in exile to make the necessary constitutional changes to relieve him of his formal authority as the head of the Tibetan community outside China.

"At this perilous moment in the history of Tibet I express complete faith in the Tibetan people. We must all hope that these inspiring changes lead to genuine freedom, happiness and prosperity for the six million brothers and sisters suffering under the Chinese tyranny."

The current Dalai Lama, Tenzin Gyatso, has progressively distanced himself from a direct political role and expressed a desire to live as a simple *monk. Next week the Tibetan community in exile will vote to elect a new* Kalon Tripa, *or prime minister.*

"Up until now foreign governments have often sought to overcome the perception of dealing with me as a political leader. Possibly they find it easier to have a formal relationship with me as an eminent religious leader. But I no longer play a political role or a pronounced spiritual role."

The Dalai Lama is revered by his followers as the 14th reincarnation of the enlightened Buddha Avalokiteshvara. The question of the spiritual succession is highly controversial and has the potential to spark serious fractures within the Tibetan community. Chinese authorities are likely to exploit any opportunities offered by the transition of power.

"Since I made my intention clear I have received repeated and earnest requests both from within Tibet and outside, to continue to provide political leadership. My desire to devolve authority has nothing to do with a wish to shirk responsibility. It is to benefit Tibetans in the long run..."

I never saw or heard any of it but somehow I do know how it all must have started. I clearly recall having read the next few words once before in a dark damp room surrounded by hills on all four sides.

"...For our people I may say my work cannot end, hence in a sense I cannot retire as long as peace needs a prose and patience needs practice. For only then can a 'human' be 'kind'."

Saturday, 7ᵗʰ August 2010

"Why can't death come from one side?" I heard the roaring of clouds from the mountain pass in the North. Just a day before my motorcycle clambered up that hill and now even a helicopter won't reach that high. "Maybe we committed a mistake by not praying at the temple of the mountain God". Tonight the mystic mountain had an expression of anger that could only be triggered by disrespect.

"Do you hear that? It's the water. A stream flooded with rain that is coming to sweep us all away." *Sahishnu* never needed a reason to whimper.

"Do I look scared? No of course not. I am not scared. I might as well go to sleep." *Tenzing* was not good at consoling. I bet he preferred to die on his motorcycle. At least he preferred to die.

Thomas was frisking his bag for another pack of the exclusive Gladiator cigarettes, "I always wanted to be rescued by a helicopter from the top of the German embassy. Apparently my dream is bound to come true." Our group assumed that he would give up smoking if he ran out of his preferred brand. It was a good night to test him. I offered him a bud from my pack.

Soon the roof got crowded. All three brothers from *Mysore* sat in a circle around the fire. Their muscles reminded me of my youth. The eldest one had a receding hairline and I am sure he was on steroids. If we were to survive that night we would need all those juiced up muscles.

Shamasheel got up and rounded us into a pyramid of sorts with the elderly Mohammedan at the centre. He took out his expensive camera and focused all of us within the frame. "Our survival is in doubt. I am sure we can capture a miscellany of sincere emotions in the last few hours of our unfulfilled lives, so do not smile for the shutter." Even in his cynical phrases he sounded brave. His gait was determinative as he entered the frame before the automatic timer chimed.

FLASH!!! CLICK!!! And we ran to see our reflections in the tiny foldable screen of *Shamasheel's* camera. I could count eleven of us. That left him out of the frame. My fear was shared by *Bardaj* who had already started shouting his name. We got no response and *Daya* went downstairs to check in our room.

"I can swear in the name of God that he was sitting right next to the chimney. He was chopping fresh dry logs to put in the fire. His brother will kill me if we cannot find him." That should have created hysteric volumes of anxiety amongst the dwellers of our roof but all I got was a bleak voice consoling me. *Atiik* sat on a chair and tried to speak as loudly as he could, "Don't get panicked, least of all because of death. We die when it is time. The only dreadful thing that can happen is that, one of our friends has gone out in the dark and damp of this unforgiving night. He will be back."

This trip was getting worse by the second. Tears were my only vent to the anger, resentment, fear and incapability that had accumulated over the last few days of the trip. I looked around and saw all the eight strangers staring right at me with tiresome eyes. They offered a patient ear.

"I use to work with my elder brother in our father's publishing house. We limited our publications to Sanskrit literature. My father was actually a learned scholar from the Sanskrit Vidyapeeth of Varanasi. He taught us that goddess Saraswati resides in our words, our hands, our books and above all in our hearts. He departed too soon. We still had a lot to learn about the industry. Consequently our printing press ran out of ink and funds. My brother had to sell the machines to pay our family loans. I considered it selling our father's virtues. And that was the last we saw of each other.

In the past two years I got married, contributed my bit to procreation and then witnessed the ugly onslaught of divorce. Money was never a problem. It hardly stuck to my hand. As it turned out I was merely a channel, borrowing money from one hand and passing it on with the other. So I even tried working as a cashier for a private firm. It took them two months to catch the boodle I managed. Since then I have been living on odd jobs and daily wages. When pockets run dry and food becomes dearer I visit my brother-in-law.

A very powerful man married my sister. He lives in Delhi. All through these years whenever I needed refuge he offered a helping hand. I clearly remember that night, though I was drunk as usual. His younger brother walked up to us. With eyes that never glanced with scepticism and a smile that was strikingly similar to his elder brother he talked deterministically. "I have to go to *Leh*, Ladakh. One of my long lost buddies is there. I want to go and surprise him." Although his younger brother was in final year of college but my brother-in-law had trust issues. As he rose from the chair he enquired, "Who all are going along with you?" Unpleasing to his ears was the answer from the other side, 'I alone will go. No other has the responsibility to take this journey. It is up to me to meet this friend of ours, talk to him and help him if possible."

It took me another hour to finish my glass of scotch and so I heard both sides of the argument. The youth in his early twenties wanted to rent a motorcycle and drive all the way up to *Leh*, Ladakh. He had been planning the trip for several months. Recently he got the news that his friend would be staying there for the weekend so it was the perfect time to visit. The picturesque mountain passes, spiralling highways and rivers overflowing with freshly melted snow gave a wake up call to my ears.

My brother-in-law was worried. Being the eldest male member of the family in a patriarchal society it was his duty to look after the younglings. A road trip half way across the country in the monsoon season was more than he could digest. In a concerned voice he said, "Look little brother I was in college once and I know the thrill of cross-country backpacking. It is not for the faint hearted. Why don't you go for a relaxing trip to Maldives or Singapore? Or even better take a cruise to some Greek island? And make sure you do have some company." These words were followed by a silence and I had a closer look at the twenty year old lad. His eyes were a blend of several shades of green, brown and blue. His hair was neatly chopped and contoured by long and thin nearly diminishing side burns. During most of the conversation I could not see his complete face as his back was towards me. "Well in any case I am all packed up and will leave tomorrow." He did not try to sound adventurous or enthusiastic.

I would have liked to sit there and gulp another bottle but the awkwardness of this argument had seeped into our conversation and my brother-in-law wanted to discuss it with me, "I am his elder brother. I know him better than he knows himself. There should be at least two individuals on such a road trip lest there is a medical emergency. Moreover he would enervate of boredom all alone on the trip. He is too young to understand the good I intend. I would have accompanied him if it was not for my business engagements." I knew neither of them would budge from their stand so I requested to be excused, "Thank you for the drinks. I have to get up early tomorrow so I will take your leave." He accompanied me to do the door for some extended greetings, "It is only 9'oclock, why leave so early? Do you have some special plans for tomorrow?"

Only men with work have plans. I am merely a baggage. But I do plan to hide for some days till I manage a new job. It is shameful I have no skills and not enough money to retire. "Brother" I added, "you must let your little brother go and if possible take a vacation with him. The two of you are lucky to have plenty and a little extra unlike most of us." God works in mysterious ways. Some words I said or probably some faces that I made prompted my brother-in-law to send me a long on this trip. He would be paying for the entire trip and all I had to do was stick like a leech. In fact I have been pretending to be a leech all my life. At first it was my father, then brother and now this young boy whose brother thinks I will look after him. Nevertheless I took the job of vouching for the little boy. I had no money. Why would I need it? God always showered his grace. I expected my brother-in-law to book return air tickets for us in the first business class flight to *Leh*.

My suitcase was absurdly overflowing. It was a week long trip and once in *Leh* I did not plan on washing my clothes.

As planned his younger brother would pick me up from my house and we would leave together. To my dismay he was in an auto rickshaw. We did not go to the airport but the local interstate bus terminal. The bus was an air conditioned Volvo and we occupied the last two seats. This bus would take us to *Manali*, our first pit stop in the road trip to *Leh*.

Bus Ride

Fridays are the most crowded on interstate buses. Almost everyone is interested in an extended weekend break. The ones who made a last minute plan had to fight for their seats. The seats in the front were occupied by backpackers from abroad. Rucksacks in neon, yellow and red were piled one above the other. The bus had a timely departure. My fellow traveller preferred to observe the highway through the window. But I knew if we were to spend ten days together I might as well get acquainted. "Excuse me. Do you two mind exchanging seats with us?" The boy sitting in front of us interrupted me just as I was about to start my conversation with *Hrijan*, "Seven of us are together and we plan to drink through the night. It would be ghastly difficult with you two sitting right in the middle of our minor commotion." *Hrijan* got up and offered his seat, "Not a problem you can have my seat but do remember this man here has quite an appetite for alcohol. He agreed to come on this trip because when my brother requested him he was totally out of his senses." The boy quickly occupied his seat, "Don't worry, we have only two bottles and there are nine of us nobody is going to overdo it." After taking his new seat *Hrijan* replied, "Oh thank you. But I do not drink. So you guys can count me out." I was glad to hear that. This meant one less portion and I think all eight of them noticed my smirk. After all it's not every day that you get a free ride to Ladakh and free booze on route

Ten minutes into the suburbs of Delhi and rain Gods got busy. The lights in the bus went out. The city-scape made way for dark desolated fields. The driver led us into believing it was his first night at work.

The highway had a mix of rickety patches which led to the first toll booth. This was our first detour. On numerous occasions I have travelled to Himachal Pradesh. The Grand Trunk Road goes straight through Haryana and Punjab for at least 400 km before we ascend for hill stations like *Manali*. Our worst fears came true when he took another high speed turn to enter into some sugarcane fields. The sugarcane was as high as our windows and constantly cluttered against the pane. This Red Bus service operating from New Delhi did not have a national permit and hence it was certain that we would be taking a detour on every check post. This was fine if we would have fallen asleep and if the trip would have taken the same time as the national highway's authorized operators do but that was not to be.

A skinny man opened the first bottle of Vodka. Each one of us put forward a glass. He looked around waited for some time and then asked us, "My window doesn't open. We must offer the first sip to *Lord Bhairo* else bad luck will follow." Even our windows were sealed and we did not know where to sprinkle the first drops of alcohol as an offering to the demon turned saint. *Hrijan* stepped up to the occasion, "Now that you have made it all so customary and consecrated I am willing to accept your first few drops of vodka." He did not have a glass. The group of seven went into a spiritual discussion. Most arguments rejected *Hrijan's* claim to the maiden sip on grounds of mortality. And then a frizzy haired boy whispered, "From the looks of it, *Hrijan* appears to be a 'Booze-Virgin' and if we treat him as a virgin sacrifice our problem is solved." Most of us agreed with him. We sacrificed *Hrijan* so that all eight of us could drink. He never asked for a refill and went off to sleep. There were fellow travellers who wanted to complain but then again an equal number of them also wanted to have a drink. Quarter to midnight and the bus stopped near a fruit whole sale market. We were asked to step down.

Most of us took this opportunity to light up our cigarettes and *Hrijan* got hold of some bananas at whole sale price. I did not have the money to buy a cigarette and *Hrijan* was my ATM. I went over to him. He offered me a banana. As we sat on the pavement looking at the conductor loading the apples, guavas, pears and oranges on to the bus I asked him, "So how was the maiden sip of vodka?" He swallowed the unchewed piece and replied, "Well it's good I only swallowed the first few drops. It had little tinge of vinegar and I knew it was already stale. In this rainy season these boys should have taken precautions. I always keep my bottles in cool and dark places." I saw him get up and had to ask, "So today was not your first drink?" He was in a hurry to get on the bus, "Oh of course it was the first time I drank today. Otherwise I drink only at my hill house in Himachal. It's cold there and my uncle gets a fresh stock of rum every season." We were destined to be punished. *Lord Bhairo* was coming for us. I sensed that rest of the journey wouldn't be pleasant. I did not share this fact with my new friends who were ignorantly sleeping. They offered me companionship, how could I let them share the burden of my sacrilege.

As the journey moved into early hours of morning we got wet and that interrupted my slumber. After all the Red-Bus service was operating second hand repaired Volvo buses. As the water trickled down my chin I peered beyond the curtains. There were at least seventy buses like ours waiting on the steep mountain road. I asked the conductor and he informed me about a landslide. We had been stuck there for past three hours. *Hrijan* was not in his seat. I looked around and his bag wasn't their either. As I walked through the aisle for the first time I felt responsibility weigh my shoulders down. I had to strain my eyes in the heavy rain to locate a roadside tea stall. Contrastingly *Hrijan* wasn't that tough to notice. He stood atop a wooden pedestal and was narrating to the mass of truck drivers and security personnel anecdotes from his life which sounded very entertaining in this rain, especially over tea and biscuits. At this rate I was sure the tea stall owner would be sold out in another hour. I stood behind the tallest man in the crowd consisting mostly of daily wage earners and seasonal labourers. Everyone was quiet so that we could hear each and every word that came out of his mouth. *Hrijan* had an emotionless voice, "You see the rain. It will end this morning. The clouds will not clear but you will have light in the morning. Enough light to turn back. The road ahead gets swampy and air gets frosty. The army is making a bridge, but don't expect it to last longer than a week. Water will pour aggressively and it will wipe out the damned and the sinned. On nights like this when we are least expecting we get the fruits of our Karma. Even the bleakest of sins are punished and if you don't want to face the consequences today leave this road and turn back where the judgment day is still far."

Nearly everyone in the crowd was above thirty. They had lived long enough to fear the consequences of their actions. No one was willing to face the repercussions today or any other day for that matter. So everyone returned to their cars, buses or trucks. They had the whole night to think. The rain stopped. It took five minutes for the tea stall to be empty again. I couldn't scold *Hrijan* but I was furious about the fact that he left the bus without informing me. We were interrupted by an old man. He wore a green turban and his grey beard contrasted with the black of the night. He held *Hrijan* by the shoulders and cried, "Ah... it has been a while since I met a young lad like you. I am sure you will not go back. Your eyes burn with a desire that cannot be stopped by obstacles hurled at you. Still I request you to rethink the time and place for such a journey." *Hrijan* picked up his bag, "Let us walk towards your vehicle. You worry a lot *Baba* but believe me the outcome of such a journey is worth the troubles." They held hands as they walked along the curved road. I had genuine worries, "We can't leave our suitcases in this bus and wander around. All of these buses look alike." *Hrijan* replied without understanding the urgency of my tone, "Then we must take our bags out. We won't be requiring this bus driver's services anymore." The old man had very little to speak and his car was parked right in front of the long lane of vehicles stalled by the landslide so he talked at a slow pace, "You may not complete this journey. Remember not all lessons come from the destination. Some chapters of your journey will fill the voids you detest." His rebuttal was rather defensive, "Void, what void? I am travelling all the way to a cold and dry desert to put some sense in to his mind. My message is sacred, urgent and completely selfless. It is a service I am offering to this friend of mine and his god forsaken community." The old man never tried to calm him down so I requested him not to shout. And he continued, "No please, do tell me *Baba* what pleasure you think I will derive from this journey? It is my money, my sweat, my time and my spiteful family that is at stake here." The old man opened up the boot of his car for our luggage as he answered, "The Photographers did not do justice to your good looks. If I may suggest, next time round publish one of the photos from your personal album." *Hrijan* took the seat next to the driver and requested a little feedback, "Now that I try publishing at least one book every year it is becoming increasingly difficult for me to interact with my readers. Thank you for your appreciation." The old man got into the driver's seat and we crawled along the mountain, "Oh I am no simple fan of your writing. I sense we are connected somehow. Upon reading your books I had these dreams where in the two of us talk." Talk he said and *Hrijan* wanted to know what they used to talk about. "Mostly you read out passages from your books. In fact if it were not for the story you told all of us at the tea stall I would have never recognized you." We were way ahead of the pack of buses now. The old gentleman was an exceptional driver and he continued his monologue, "However you never mentioned in that book the date of your travel. If it would have not been for this landslide we would have never met." *Hrijan* lowered the window and whispered, "Those dreams won't haunt you anymore. Now that you have conveyed his message to me I am sure he will leave you alone. Be thankful for I am here to deliver a Carte blanche." The breeze after a rainstorm smells of the grainy earth. It soothes the olfactory senses and before you realize you fall asleep. *Hrijan* was safely tucked behind the seat belt and I am sure he did not hear the old man's last few words that night, "Son I pray he grants you freedom as well, though you still have a long way to go."

Manali

That night was a tough journey and I barely remember when I fell asleep. Maybe it was when one of the snake shaped roads entered a long and dark tunnel. Although the ride was bumpy especially after the rains, but we were too tired to complain and I slept like a baby. Not much has been written about *Manali*. Of course school and college camping trips are very common but seldom do we read or hear about a flirtation with nature that begins in this affordable weekend getaway. The morning was very bright. *Hrijan* had two cups of tea in his hands and offered me one of them. The old man had already finished his drink and was having breakfast now. Hastily we grabbed some sandwiches for the road. We were very grateful to this elderly man. He tried his best to make up for the time lost in the landslide, however we reached *Manali* at around three in the afternoon so inevitably we had to waste the rest of the day in a motel. The tourist season was over. Our room was inexpensive and rather luxurious. Consequently I had no plans of leaving the bed for the rest of the day. At first I considered taking a bath. Then again my weary bottom had a pretty valid argument. All I had to do was lie still in my bed for the whole night. Who needs a bath for that? Once *Hrijan* piled up the suitcases in a corner and changed into a comfortable pair of flip flops we were supposed to be ready.

"*Astitva*, are you ready to explore this town? Wear something warm and comfortable. I am waiting downstairs", he said hurriedly.

I tried to explain, "Hold on *Hrijan*. You know, how we have been travelling for over a day now and tomorrow would begin early as well.

So I was just wondering wouldn't it be a better idea to sit tight in the room and gain some calories for the road ahead?"

His reply was prompt, "Did I tell you about *Beas*?" No he hadn't ever mentioned anyone named *Beas* and he continued, "My ancestral village is located at the foothills of Karakoram range. The very same river that flows in the outdoors of *Manali* provides for our village. Now you tell me, wouldn't it make perfect sense for me to pay my tribute to the ever benevolent river God *Beas*." The snow white bed sheets crumbled as I hesitantly walked over them. The window overlooked this *Beas*, the almighty river God of his. The woods were cramped with tourist excursions on the far side of the bank. Holy or not but the water did seem inviting.

The sky was clear and shone like a blue sapphire. The water mirrored the same. I could comfortably sleep in the open. My plans to get some shut eye contradicted with *Hrijan's* adventures. So I waited under a tree while he went for a holy dip. Every single second that I spent amongst those trees was longer than an entire city day. Children of the poor herdsmen who reared animals for wool and meat were chasing rabbits in the garden adjacent to the main gate. Imperfectly shaped leaves dropped from the trees to paint the grass in mural shades of green and yellow. The city was a big fading dream for me now. I swear I could lie on that grass for at least the rest of this trip, if not my entire life and then suddenly a sound from the city woke me up. My eyes were greeted with another visual from the city. The tourists had gathered around a giant stone on the right bank and were cheering two men. They were on opposite banks and were holding ropes fastened around two pulleys. The man on the far bank appeared to be a foreigner. He had a camera and would occasionally leave the rope and take some pictures of the river. The crowd had their cameras out too. I had to hustle my way forward. Once there all I could make out was that something tied by the rope was submerged in the centre of the river and these men were holding it in its place. The foreigner would adjust his cap every time he was pulled down by the weight of the object in the water. I looked around to find *Hrijan*. He must not miss this spectacle. Then a local boy standing next to the huge rock gave a signal to the foreigner on the far bank. Both of them stepped back and started lashing with the rope furiously and in the process sending tremors across the whole length of the rope which coadunated right in the centre. I took out my camera to capture whatever was in the water. The crowd stopped cheering. The water was cold and a constant chilly breeze sent shivers down my spine. But he was glowing in all shades of red, pink and white. *Hrijan* was not missing anything; he was right in the centre of it all. This boy had a harness around his waist, both his hands gripped the ropes from either side firmly and his clothes were I think on the other side of the bank. He looked straight into the skies; immuned to the cheers and jeers amongst the crowd. Freezing water splattered all around as he rose to at least ten feet above the river before closing his eyes and joining his hands in prayer. Once again as he took the holy dip the crowd silenced. Ladies were horror struck, children were amused and one man was at peace. The spectacle lasted for several minutes before *Hrijan* pulled his way to the other side of the river. He looked tired. The foreigner hugged him tightly with a towel. They sat on the other side for some time and I came back to my bed of grass under the tree...

When it rains in the hills a bowl of *Thupka* comes to your rescue. We were joined by the foreigner. He was in his early thirties. He was still adjusting his cap as we shook our hands. "So you must be *Astitva*. *Hrijan* has not told me much about you but I guess we are old enough to introduce ourselves. My name is Thomas Mueller." He took the seat right beside me. He had big green eyes behind a pair of frameless spectacles. I looked at the menu and the prices. They were not reasonably priced but surely I wasn't going to pay so I ordered the most expensive dish. While we waited for the food to come I tried to stir the conversation towards a less remorseful topic but in vain. Both of them were interested in his job. "I work in the mutual fund consultancy of Deutsche Bank in Berlin. What do you do *Astitva*?" Isn't it perfectly normal for a man to be unemployed? Why is it that one is always defined by his profession? He could have asked about my family, however even that talk would have not lasted for more than a minute. Luckily I have been reading and a simple reply to such an inevitable query has been found, "Thomas, I am in between jobs. This is also the reason why I had time to travel to *Leh*." *Hrijan* took the salad bowl and added, "To the best of my knowledge this trip was very much forced upon you by my brother. You never mentioned you were enjoying the responsibility." Surprisingly Thomas came to my rescue, "Oh I know exactly what he means. See I had a week long break between two scheduled client meetings so I took the time to travel to *Leh*. I have booked a return flight from Srinagar to Delhi". This also gave me a chance to change the topic, "So you will be travelling with us to *Leh* and then go on to Srinagar. It is good to know I have someone my own age with me. Being a baby-sitter is not the best job in the world you know." On that note we walked back to our hotel. Thomas would spend the night with us. He had a splendid pair of beige cargos with more pockets than my rucksack. Inevitably I kept on wondering about the robust and utility based German garments. The room was on the third floor. *Hrijan* retired immediately on the soft bed. Thomas opened up his bag and brought out a bottle of beer. I jumped across to the other side of the bed to fetch an empty glass. He was too courteous to say no. I did think of contributing some money for the drinks, but then again I would have to ask *Hrijan* for it, and he was already asleep. Even I wanted to retire but a free glass of beer needed to be cherished in the moonlight. I will never understand why a man needs a bottle by his side to enjoy the gift of nature. My eyes couldn't fathom the limitless skies above and I drowned my limitations in that glass of chilled beer. Peace seldom lasts in modern times and I heard shouting and swearing downstairs. In the garden below were all those boys we met in the bus. I waved my hand from the third floor. They recognised me although they were too drunk to upstage a conversation. I went downstairs to meet them. They were all dressed up to dazzle the local discotheque. *Manali* is a small town. The next day involved a lot of travelling. *Leh* was still an odd five hundred kilometres. Perhaps this party would make the remaining journey less exhaustive.

The disco had sub woofers but no jockey. It had foldable chairs but no bar stools. The city had rain and the disco did not have a roof. We were literally dancing in a tent house with no dedicated dance floor. The food was something we did not experiment with. Instead we searched for the company of the opposite sex. There was not much male competition either. My gaze dotted upon a damsel over at the counter. She seemed shy and was not drinking. How would I pay for a drink? *Hrijan* would never lend me money. Even these boys accompanying me here behaved miserly when it came to spending on girls at a disco. "Would you dance with me?' Seemed a more economical option and she readily agreed. The music was repetitive, loud and racy. Her eyes were small, petite and she had a flattened nose. The lipstick was in a gauche shade of red. In fact her disfigured features reminded me of my wife. Blaring speakers urged us to come close and I strained my ears to hear her whispers, "Which hotel are you staying at?" Of course local people did not frequent this place. Though from past experience I knew where our conversation would take us. On any other day it would be my room but not today. So I asked her, "How about we do this in your hotel room? Her hands lost their grip on my shoulder and she went over to the bar tender. This time a smile minced her face when she answered, "That will cost you an extra three hundred rupees."

Never in my life have I slept with a woman and paid for it. That night was no exception. I ought to have seen this coming. The signs were quite clear. My clothes were a disgrace to party culture; I seemed too drunk to walk leave alone dance or perform in bed; never did I mention how great her hair was done and there was no shady walk under the moon. Money was the only reason a girl would agree to get involved with me in such a scenario and I did not have enough."

Chores

Daya had come upstairs with *Hrijan* long ago. *Hrijan* must have heard everything, though it was impossible to make out any change of emotions on *Hrijan's* face. (Even if he had one I cared the least.)

"You're sitting very close to the fire. Please don't expect me to baby-sit you all the time," *Daya* dragged his feet next to mine, "So are you regretting not sleeping with that woman? From where I stand it is very much possible that none of us will get the company of the fairer sex anytime soon." He was not kidding but he was not upset either. He shifted the pedestal of attention away from me and in a rather loud squeaking voice spoke to all of us,

"Although most of you present here are in possession of a faultlessly developed set of limbs and wits, but without the assistance of an entire class of men like me your so called utopia would be unsustainable. Most of us are scared to die tonight because tomorrow might have held the key for a brighter future. Perhaps tomorrow would come with a hope of reconciliation with a forgotten one. Or the scheduled meeting would open doors to a whole new avenue of premium privileges. The most dispirited amongst us folk must be those who saved every penny over the last year to fund this unfortunate trek into the unchartered town of *Leh*. *Astitva* says he will miss a female companion but I have never experienced a woman's touch. To be very frank I do not envy *Astitva* because in these two days I have served Man to the best of my capabilities. The funny part is it all started as a chore. Most of the guests in this motel are asleep when I wake up. Last night I got a head start with *Bardaj*. He rarely interrupts my five hour slumber but something was unusual about the sky that night. There is no window in my quarter. So I sat next to the common room window on the ground floor. The Moon God took a night off and the stars were hiding behind those grey clouds of sadness. The rocky mountain side had this small but overbearing dwarf cloud that seemed to caveat about an impending onslaught. With a roar from the West and a thud from the South it all poured down. We had orders to shut our doors and windows even on the slightest indication of a shower. At that hour of night it seemed cynical to go to each room and request all of you, our guests to shut the windows. So I sat next to the reception just in case we had any further notification from the authorities. Possibly the next gulp of air traversing with the wind brought down water which smelt of Mother Earth and all shades of green and brown. That sweet smelling breeze slipped into my poncho and whispered a lullaby to finally put me to sleep. *Bardaj* ji had a bucket in his left hand and a mug in the right with which he knocked my sleepy head, "Take the first crack. We have some work to do mate." On rubbing my eyes the picture of our *Sahib* became vivid. Bucket was blue and mug was mauve. As I stood up from the seat I felt my poncho get wet. There was water in my boots. Some of it damped the carpet. A whole lot of it filled the lobby. *Sahib* handed me the mug. I walked across the aisle to my quarter. Usually my days start with a bath and fresh pair of clothes. As one might have guessed we hardly come across any designer boutiques in the border town of *Leh*. Nevertheless I have gathered an assortment of fashion labels over the years. Most of the guests leave some ill fitting or torn clothes or simply misplace their rags. Though my wardrobe was not in vogue with the latest trends but it did offer a variety of clothes. Today however I had little choice.

The floor gave way and rain water drenched my mother's photograph poised on the table next to the bed. For the first time I was happy my room did not have a view. That reminded me of all the guests with their windows, chimneys and balconies. *Sahib* was already on the roof. The skies were dark, unlike any morning I have seen in my time in *Leh*. Firewood was wet. By lanes were clean, for the very first time there were no polythene bags, no tobacco stains, and no dusty roads. All was drenched and enveloped in an all-engulfing water stream. One could walk to the grocery store but swimming would get you there faster. The chimney was overflowing. It had an outlet on every floor. *Sahib* went down the staircase. "The phone lines are out of order. My brother will come here in the morning. If he finds this place water logged I am sure to lose my share of the will." For the first time in thirteen years he cried and I sat next to him. "Every year I work in this motel for eight months. This motel has been my life ever since terrorist and army made it impossible for us to live in our house boats." His eyes gave glimpses of a crimson hue, "Now Allah wants to take this sole abode away as well."

Thirteen years and I eat everyday with this man. Sometimes in penultimate winter months we even share a room. He lets me sleep on the ground. His only expectation from me is to toil for him relentlessly. When he has guests from the Kashmir valley he purposefully talks with them in Koshur. Obviously when they laugh it is because I am an object of amusement. My dark skin and a lineage that has never produced an impactful historical champion grant them the right to amuse themselves over my tiresome fate. My brothers and fathers travelled to far out districts of India in search of work. Where ever we settle, it is the miserly pay and menial jobs that await us. I had every reason to fleece this morning. Workers from Bihar could easily find employment in the unorganised sector. However revolt is not in our blood. Not today and not when this man needs all the hands in the world I decided not to leave *Sahib* alone. With that mauve coloured mug of mine and a blue bucket we sat on the staircase. *Sahib* hugged me before he asked for my hand to lift him up. We started from the top floor lobby. As I looked through the door that led to the roof a cloud cover urged me to give *Sahib* the much needed hollow assurance, "The rain will stop. We will wait." Today I needed to inspire this gentleman, "Have I told you how thirsty I get when you wake me up early?" I made *Sahib* smile with me instead of laugh at me. Both of us removed the stripped pyjamas which hadn't been washed for months; rubber slippers were necessary to prevent any chance of electrocution; and most importantly we decorated our faces with a smile. The same smile that shone on *Sahib's* face when he checked in the first guests."

With his robust attitude he need not sit near the bonfire. More of us needed to be warm. *Daya* walked up to the old man and enquired, "Should I get some hot tea for you." The eldest among us was the most respected and his placate was of prime importance. Quite naturally he was also the calmest. But he insisted, "*Daya* we all want to hear in detail about the night that sneaked upon us while we hoisted some fancy dreams in cushioned beds."

So he continued, "We started with the conference room on the top floor. *Sahib* was quick on guidance and I tried to work my hands as quickly as his words, "God forbid *Daya* but if we had to offer refuge to any new customers this room could accommodate plenty." Indeed as we talk right now a whole family of eight sleeps there with three children and an infant. Huge wide windows on three sides were opened. One by one we filled our buckets and emptied the water on to the alley. In the absence of a carpet we were less cautious and a lot quicker. That reminds me, we spend a fortune on the upkeep of our carpets. *Sahib* says some of them were woven by his grandmother back in the Valley. As much as we wanted to save them, drying them was indeed troublesome. Firewood was damp and the Sun had no plans of entertaining us. So *Sahib* wrapped up the lot on the second floor and stacked it up with the curtains I enfolded from the first floor. Another hour and we were down to the ground floor. Unsurprisingly all the water that we wiped from the floors above had accumulated here. Consequently *Bhaiyas* from Mysore were awake. One of them was standing at the reception waiting for some assistance. I rushed to their room. The elderly gentleman was still sleeping in his wet bed. The youngest of his sons was standing on a chair placing the last of their suitcases on the top bunk of the cabinet. An unusual greeting awaited me, "You are rather late. I hope you had a pleasant sleep." I walked over with the bucket in my hand and he continued, "Surely we will need plenty of those buckets if you want to save this city of yours. The travel agent never said anything about a storm season in *Leh*." Here I feel obliged to assure each and every one of you, in the thirteen years of my life that I have spent here never have I seen a drop plummet from the skies. I suppose it was the *Bhaiya* with golfer's shoulders who was scared the most. Certain vexation in his voice suggested so, "This better not be some plumbing problem. I will sue you and your boss for torturing us the whole night. Do you have any idea that those trousers were from the house of Dolce and Gabbana." Honestly being a farmer from *Bihar* working as an odd-job-man in a motel in *Leh* I had no idea where this Dolce & Gabbana lived. I assume *Bhaiya* must be visiting them quite often in the big city. If you tell them that you got the clothes wet in a flood they might not get mad at you, rather they would be concerned about your well being. Moreover you shouldn't have taken it from their house in the first place. Come to think of it, if their house is so big that they hardly notice a missing pair of trousers then maybe if we all lived in Dolce or Gabbana's house then none of us would get wet. The carpets would be dry. Curtains would be colourful and sheeted from rain dripped windows. Maybe in another life I would like to be born in this wonderful house of Dolce & Gabbana."

Boys from Mysore were humble or the last day had taught them humility. The youngest one offered his hand and an apology to *Daya*, "Pray the last words we ever exchange are not of sorrow and grief. I will interrupt and say sorry to you right now because when we depart this land for a better place with Allah I would thank you for being with me and my brothers till the end." *Daya* was a short man of anorexic built but that moment when he stood next to the fire his shadow encased me. It did not make me feel ashamed of my silhouette but proud to share my last few days with a selfless hireling. Remaining occupants of the motel were fast asleep when this happened so we listened intently as *Daya* continued his discourse, "There were eight hands on the ground floor and just one bucket. Apparently the lobby morphed in to a mini swimming pool which had several outlets - one main door leading to a steep flight of steps and a window each on the East and the West walls. *Sahib* dragged the bucket across the floor till it became heavy even to lift off the floor and *Bhaiya* ploughed the mauve mug in the opposite direction. My hands were empty and pushing the water with bare hands would have been too imaginative or heroic. Instead I looked to *Atiik* for improvisation. He never disappoints anyone and returned from his room with a beer jug. He had questions for *Sahib*, "Did you take out the fuse from the meter room? With all this water around anyone could get a shock." Now how come this never occurred to *Sahib*? He could have got the two of us killed. *Bardaj* replied promptly, "Soon after the rainstorm lights went out. The T.V. in my room and fridge in the kitchen are not functioning. We do need electricity to get electrocuted." My boss is a smart man. He had of course thought about the situation from every point of view. After an hour the soles of my feet began to wrinkle. When the clock struck four in the morning the lines on my palm read an illegible destiny. The brothers from Mysore exchanged turns with the mug. Elder brother had sweaty arms and droplets traced the veins on his wheatish complexion. Youngest *Bhaiya* strained his forehead ahead of all others by walking up and down shouting, screaming and ripping his fluffy hair off. *Atiik* sat next to the door and observed his sons. A new tuft of hair turned grey on his chest as he saw those men rip their T-shirts apart with muscles best suited to butchering. Skies were thundering above us and the drainage pipes under us were trembling with overwhelming quantity of water that the rain had brought. A very gentle fear gripped us. We trembled in unison with the roar of the gushing stream as it flowed past the motel. Nobody ever thought about giving up. One handful of the morning's pour at a time till the time we emptied it all. Four hours and Three hundred twenty eight pints of beer later we had our motel back. It looked stained and sent off olfactory signals resembling a compost pit. *Sahib* fell face first on the couch in the lobby and the brothers from Mysore lay exhausted in their room, *Atiik* walked up to me and with a polite smile requested, "Staying awake all night does not add to my ailing health. Even the boys could use some tea now. So how about you make some for all of us." *Sahib* agreed with him, "Do ask others who are awake if they also want some tea or coffee. Remember to append it in their bill before you start cooking." The kitchen is on the first floor so on my way upstairs I kept the kettle to boil. *Hrijan* and *Astitva* were still asleep. Thomas *Sahib* preferred coffee and *Tenzing* wanted milk. Milk reminded me of the fridge. Nothing was left over from the previous night. *Sahib* was slumbering on the couch so I asked *Atiik* for some money, "It will be deducted from your bill. For now I need it to buy milk from the grocery store. The local milkman has not come yet." Looking at all the tiring faces he did not hesitate in giving some advance, moreover he sent his youngest son with me. "It is not wise to travel alone", he said.

As we crossed the second street of cobblestone the Sun was above our heads. Tourists were on either side of the road wearing their favoured eye gear or head gear. Hard to notice at first but it seemed as though there was a pattern. Beelines on either side were directed in opposite directions. In fact one could say that the jaywalkers on the left were visiting a tourist spot while the ones on the right were returning back; it could be the other way round also. The grocery store near our motel was still closed. In fact most shops near about were closed, hence we walked to *Tsang's* shop. The main road stretching from the mosque towards the old *Leh* bus stop curved along the slope. The mosque had an unusual amount of devotees for a Friday morning. *Bhaiya* figured they were preparing for the special afternoon prayers. Perhaps *Bhaiya* did not pay attention to the faces in the paved courtyard beyond the mosque. There were French blondes from the hotel two blocks away from ours; dressed in local attire were ladies who talked in some oriental accent, refugees from the Kashmir Valley sat next to their Tibetan counterparts. All had their backs towards the midrib of the mosque. We were in quite a hurry and pushed people all around us yet nobody minded our elbowing. *Bhaiya* was sceptical, "What if even your friend's shop is closed?" This was a baseless fear because *Tsang* lived in a single storey house just behind the shop, "*Bhaiya* even if his shop is closed he wouldn't mind opening the shutters especially for us. For the past eleven years the two of us have had evening drinks together every Saturday night. *Jigma*, his wife must be mopping the floor right now. Though they have a small shop but they maintain proper hygiene." *Sahib* preferred to buy the daily essentials from shops owned by refugees from the Kashmir valley but we had no option today. As we took the next left at the T-junction the road not only curved but it also caved in until we could walk no further.

There was no shop and no house behind the shop. Three security personnel, an ambulance and several tourists stood between us and the five bodies on the ground. Reaction would have been to run away from *Bhaiya* and towards the family of five that lay in the debris but nerve endings on my hair responded differently. Faces of the deceased were not recognizable and even after spending last eleven years with them I had to ask who they were. Praying to hear names that did not rhyme with *Tsang* and *Jigma*. *Tsang* had a little daughter. She had her hand stuck in a cookie jar so the medics had to cut it from the elbow to carry the body out. Improbable as it may sound but *Tsang's* brother also died that night. He must have come to spend the weekend and ask for his share in the property. Both of their playful childhoods would be futile if the last words that they exchanged were an argument over a piece of land. *Bhaiya* held my right arm and dragged me along to the end of the road which was not far considering the road had a huge crater. The local peace keeping forces, the border security personnel, the Indian army, several cranes and an odd hundred youth were attempting to recover from the rubbles, remains of a refugee haven. To our left was the queue of 'gentlemen and ladies' swarming to see the devastating facade of nature while the queue on the opposite side of the road was returning to their sanctuaries. On one side were tourists excited to see a crater in the all bearing mountain while the other had men disheartened by a tear in the cities heart. Shutterbugs were heard trying to save these moments forever for the stone faced hearts of men who found this catastrophe to be an adventurous memory while others burdened their soul with horrors of a fateful night which will haunt the city for generations to come. "Do you see men dragging bodies of other men?" *Bhaiya* pointed to the remains of a bustling city centre. While I stood on my toes to look that far the most engaging act of helpfulness was on display just beneath our feet. "*Bhaiya* I am sure I saw *Hrijan* there." The security forces had a perimeter around the whole crater. Towards the right a narrow ramp led us downstairs where *Hrijan* was sitting on the rubble in his pyjamas. *Bhaiya* recognised him and looked puzzled, "*Daya* you told us he was slumbering in his room unaware of this allusion, possibly dreaming of a wonderland." I can swear his room was locked from inside, so I inferred he must be fast asleep. *Bhaiya* sat facing him, "You look like you could use a hand." *Hrijan* was separating men from matter very patiently. He looked back at us with an expression that did not deliver any grief. In a group of five he was digging the ruins. The blood on his shirt got me worried and I asked him, "Shouldn't you be on your bed wrapped in the cosy sheets of our deluxe room?" We honestly did not plan on intruding the relief work but he left his shovel and got up. He requested the remaining four members to continue digging and he promised to return soon. They nodded back. *Hrijan* spoke in a mellow voice with overtones of decree, "Look around you. Does this remind you of a deluxe room in pleasure valley? Right where you stand was a school. *Hasaan* sits upon the keystone of the primary school where I was to volunteer as an English teacher. Is there anywhere else that I would rather be right now?" He looked up; not at the rain Gods but at the flocks of tourists taking pictures of the relief work and continued, "You offer me a hand, and I could use all the hands around me which are preoccupied in capturing the remorse of this day on film. For the first time in my life I am drenched in blood that is not my own. I lifted three bodies this morning. The army official says they lifted thirty more. By noon I guess we will stack up hundreds of them." My hand was on his shoulders but they were not tensed at all I guess he wasn't responding to us. He had a lot to say and I did not interrupt, "This boy who lived in the same street as the school was covered in mud. You know he had a smile on his face when we recovered his body. I presume he died in his sleep."

Hasaan could not understand the numbness in *Hrijan's* eyes, "Surely that is a gentle way to die" *Bhaiya* consoled him, "preferable to most men."

To this comment we got a response, "He was nine years old. Is that a preferable age to die? He wanted an extra chocolate from me and I refused him. I said it would be unfair to his classmates. He would not take no for an answer and snatched the chocolate. *"Life is Unfair"* he said before disappearing in to the swarm of school kids."

My handkerchief was already wet from the last night's flood so I couldn't wipe his tears. Eventually *Bhaiya* used words to condole him, "This is not your fault. Stop punishing yourself. How could have you made any difference? It is a natural calamity. Don't hold yourself responsible for these deaths." Expression on *Hrijan's* face changed from gloom to grave, "Of course I am not responsible for my fellow men. Maybe I should go back to the hotel with you and also take some pictures while I am at it. Do me a favour, leave me alone. Last night was a natural calamity but I can do a lot today. Who knows how many more daughters and sons are waiting for my hands to lift them off this earth?" We walked away with our backs towards the rubble of human hearts. The wailing voices had died out. Retaliation was in full swing and the crater was the bureau of men with a zest to rise from a great fall. "Hey stop." *Hrijan* wanted to say something, "Actually you can give me a hand. Will you take a friend of mine along with you back to the hotel?" He was asking me, "His name is *Sahishnu*. We departed *Manali* together. Last night when the floods came, he was hiding in the mosque with his elder brother. He is sitting next to the missing persons counter right now." Of course we agreed. *Sahib* had a miserly heart but an extra customer wouldn't be difficult to accommodate in his grand motel.

Sahishnu was wearing a fancy pair of pants. He sat on a plastic stool and from the first impression it was hard to believe that he could qualify to be anyone's sibling. In late twenties I guess he seemed rather scared for a Marathi statesman. His introduction did not take long, "My name is *Sahishnu*. How are you? Lucky for me that *Hrijan* and you all survived last night." It was the epilogue that lasted our entire journey back to the motel, "*Hrijan* is very gracious. I was sure he would send someone for me. Hopefully you have something to eat back at the motel." He had been traumatized after spending the last night in a mosque and losing his elder brother, so I restrained from being impolite but *Bhaiya* wanted to know about last night. He put it rather bluntly, "Sorry to hear about your brother's demise. He might not even receive a proper funeral but I am sure he took good care of you last night." *Sahishnu* halted in the middle of the road and stared back at the remnants. I whispered my condolence, "I am sorry. Don't look back. It is all over." *Sahishnu's* eyeballs bounced from *Bhaiya* to me and back again before he exploded, "Are you under the impression that my brother is dead? Well gentlemen indeed we had a gruelling night. Readily my brother would have sacrificed for me, but nothing of that sorts happened. You can wipe the poignancy off your faces, actions speak louder much louder. We left the action behind us. Men like my brother and *Hrijan* are down there," he said pointing towards the hallowed old city, "You see no grief on their faces because they are engineers of the future. Dismay comes to us fairly naturally while they churn the chagrin into effort. As *Hrijan* strikes the ground with his shovel he prays to find only bricks and dust because rubble never added to a death count. My brother moves his pen slowly because every name that he appends is not merely a record, but a son, a father, a brother that has been lost. I see them work with one thousand two hundred army personnel tirelessly and I observe it is their collective will that feeds the zest to work. So if it is sympathy that you have inside of you, lock it up. Need of the hour is an appetite to empathize the graveness and prepare."

"Prepare for what?" I ask and he says, "There is a storm coming."

We returned without milk. The water in the kettle had evaporated by then, though it must have whistled for us to come once or twice. Unsure if anyone was listening."

⌒❦⌒

Journey Cut Short

Maybe I know who that kettle was. Or maybe there were a lot of kettle-heads on that roof ready to come apart or already blustered. The consequence was not as unfussy as the kettle. If only we could all just evaporate the fervour bubbling inside us. *Hrijan* had moved away from the fire. His eyes fixed at the monastery. *Shamasheel* was also observing the same monastery but he was vocal, "Look at the long line of cars heading to that monastery. I am sure they have supplies to last several nights." He was not the only one who wished he was up there. Thomas stood next to *Hrijan* with his favourite cigarette. They were looking at the mountain and holding hands, till one of them laughed. I am sure it wasn't funny. The sheer act of staring at the same mountain before death could make you laugh. "We went up that hill once before. If I am to die tonight I would have gone to many more such places." The voice was coarse, unlike any leader preceding him. As a matter of fact most leaders of Tibetan independence are not even half the orators their global counterparts are. Tonight he would get the much needed practice because he led the discourse hence forth.

"I shall share with all of you not a place but the journey to that place. We never reached our destination. From where I see that is not a failure however it is hard to walk in *Hrijan's* shoes. We returned half way from his friend's place. Early as we left we were greeted by a refreshing morning drizzle. As the highways arched up the mountain there was no dust at all. *Hrijan* took off his helmet and led our pack. There was a beam on his face. Anyone would be blessed to have a friend like him. I am sure on the other side of those mountains, where that old friend of his lived, there were equally enthusiastic preparations for our arrival. Though not much had been said about this friend, from the brief description I had received it was clear that not even *Astitva*, who was accompanying *Hrijan*, had met this friend of his. They always referred to him as an old friend. The ride from *Manali* to *Leh* had been long and tiring. This escalation was different; we were not in a hurry to cover up lost time nor were the roads jam packed with tourists. Several shops on either side of the road were selling special rain coats and gum boots. After half an hour I had my first halt at a check post where my two-day travelling pass was examined and duly stamped, but these two did not stop. They were too keen racing each other. I saw them slow down but that was once they reached atop the army camp checking the passes. They were waiting for me. The rest of the road was very steep. Drizzle had started to wet our jackets. My attire was perfect for the travel while *Hrijan* and *Astitva* were travelling in fancy clothes that did little to ward off the pouring that had started. Although I advised them to suit up at one of those shops but it seems *Hrijan* was too eager to cross the mountain pass and reach *Nubra valley*. Once there we planned to stay for a night but *Hrijan* was not carrying clothes. He always claimed to be the best prepared and he said, "My friend will offer me new clothes. Divine shades of red, yellow, maroon. If my word gets through to him I might as well get a haircut. Then life would be simple." *Astitva* observed the route closely to reach the conclusion that he must lead us. He ordered *Hrijan* to wear his helmet. *Astitva* was more experienced than me and *Hrijan* so we followed the zigzag path chalked by his tires on the muddy road. The road was not always like this. The gravel made way for the Earth over several months of snowfall and subsequent melting. It got cold pretty soon. My fingers were getting wet and slowly became numb. They were stuck to the brakes on the right handle. Ever since I learnt how to ride a bicycle I prefer to use the hind brakes. They gently slow you down and can be used frequently. On the hills we hardly got to speed up. The clutch on my left was out of reach for most of the morning. When we were very lucky we got to hit the second gear at a modest 25km/hr.

Leh is a valley. All around were mountains that shrouded this valley. The city was an arid brown scope while these mountains were a lush green escape. Parched foothills were a recent history, our present traced soggy green wild pastures into a future swathed in whitish clouds which dwelled on the distant peaks. Mountains offered their first novel fauna in herds of yak that grazed these feral pastures. Unlike rest of the milch family, one finds them fittingly dressed for an unwieldy winter. We slowed down to absorb the landscape but I seriously believe *Astitva* was busy envying their woolly coats. On the far corner of the road sitting in his car was an elderly gentleman. He shouted at me, "Would you be kind enough to ask your friend not to go near the herd." He had a paintbrush in his hand and a canvas in his car. His dulcet words of complaint betrayed a fountainhead of art. We were in a hurry and the old gentleman needn't worry about our intrusion. Somehow *Hrijan* couldn't help but touch what pleasured his eyes. So when I turned around he was sitting next to a baby. Baby girl I suppose because it was beautiful with brown hair. But then again it could have been a boy because it had hair all over. The horns had just sprouted and it was clumsily eating from *Hrijan's* hand. All my doubts about the yak's gender lay to rest when the baby allowed *Hrijan* to hug it. He has always had his way with the fairer sex. Probably the herd had no natural predator, otherwise they wouldn't let a baby wander outside the herd. Despite of me sneaking the last few yards the baby yak got scared and ran away. A wiggly baby yak running all over a pasture is an adorable sight comparable to an infant's first few steps. He had a tiny bushy tail and a hairstyle resembling one of the boys from a rock band. Though *Astitva* was not a pet lover but even he wanted to take the baby yak home. Our faces had a smile accredited to the novel sight of the endearing baby but *Hrijan* looked concerned. Maybe he was upset because the baby ran away when I joined their chit-chat. *Astitva* was sitting next to the artist in his car. We walked over and saw a nearly complete composition of the untamed slopes. *Astitva* looked so excited, "This will make for a splendid memory. We can hang it in our living room." *Hrijan* was uninterested. He looked away at the pastures and replied with a sigh, "It will only bring bad luck. Look at the herd. All the yaks are black in colour except our baby yak." *Hrijan* walked back to his motorcycle and gazed at the bedimmed sky.

Most of Tibetans are familiar with this superstition. Any unique coloured yak in a herd is a bad omen. *Hrijan* went closer to the herd in order to make sure that the baby belonged to the herd. Our bottoms shivered as the engines roared to gasp air. The artist promised *Astitva* he would showcase the painting in his shop. Upon returning from Nubra valley he could collect the same from the tiny settlement near *Spituk*. With escalation the air got thinner, breathing got intensified and the greenery receded like *Astitva*'s hairline. This hinted to the arrival of the rocky patch which had a grey shade that contrasted with the snowy scalp of the mountain. Two months ago these would have been covered in snow and two months hence they will be covered in snow. Such is the execrable weather of this mountain pass. Aloof from the surrounding hoary rocks were puddles of shimmery silver platter. Pallid neck of the mountain God had ornaments around it, befitting its majestic presence. Far and wide as they maybe two tarns occupied much of our photographs. *Sankar* was the closest we got to one of these merest. "Is it water? Indeed it is. Recently melted snow chilled by the clammy weather" exclaimed *Hrijan*. No algae atop the surface of luminous water dazzling with the brilliance of unsettled serenity. He continued, "I wonder how it tastes. I wonder if it's cold. I wonder if it's as holy as the Ganges." Little did we know that all his questions would soon be answered?

While our second stop was attributed to spell bounding fauna the next pit stop alarmed our diminishing adrenaline levels. *Hrijan* halted us by waving his hand. He got off the motorcycle and removed his helmet to reveal a red nose. I was worried because he was asphyxiating, "You don't look so good. Is it the wind or the altitude? Are you on some sort of medicine?" He rested his back against the mountain and spoke with gushes of air, "What does it look like? Have you heard about Rudolph the red nose reindeer? Well apparently my nose is frozen just like his. I was breathing with my mouth open." *Astitva* was very reluctant as he gave the solution, "Maybe we should return and come tomorrow with our rain coats." *Hrijan* did not let him complete the sentence, "These are two-day passes we are carrying in our bags, which cost a lot. And it takes one whole day to get them issued. There is no turning back. I will just catch my breath and then we proceed." He reminded me of a wounded King Gesar, the most decorated warrior of Tibetan history. The boy was so overwhelmed with a desire to unite with an old friend that he declared pain to be transitory. Even as he sat counting each breath with a vehicle passing by, he always faced the valley, his destination. "Once we reach the top of this mountain I guess we could take some rest" I suggested. This was enough for *Hrijan* to gear up again for the road that was yet to be fathomed. He got on his motorcycle and looked me in the eyes before elaborating, "You are right *Tenzing*. I won't need this helmet anymore. Now if I just ride behind that truck I can breathe with my mouth wide open." I should have returned a glance but *Astitva* already mounted his bike. Few days ago we were narrowly escaping landslides with our blistering speed and today I was a part of this slow moving caravan, nevertheless this caravan would not walk backwards."

Tenzing was still halfway through his dialogue when Mr. *Kadar*, the owner of our guest house honked his car furiously. His brother enquired from the roof itself and the old gentleman replied, "*Bardaj* I am leaving for *Srinagar*. A very important business has come up, so I leave you in-charge." A leer was visible on one side of *Bardaj's* face. Thomas responded with an ardent smile when he heard the word *Srinagar*. He ran downstairs and requested Mr. *Kadar* to take him along, "See I have booked my airplane ticket from Srinagar to Delhi. There is no need for me to rot with this lot on the rooftop." The owner was a very enterprising man and he announced to all others as well, "Under the dark shadow of recent ruinous events I offer my services to anyone who wishes to travel to Srinagar. Most of you want to reach back home before Sunday and that is very much possible if you take a flight from the capital of Kashmir." There was a new avenue to save our souls. I wanted to know *Hrijan's* opinion but he was not interested. It appeared the fact that he failed to meet his friend had dismayed him from any chance of survival. *Shamasheel* answered Mr. *Kadar*, "Indeed very generous of you. But we have already booked our plane tickets from *Leh*, each costing twenty thousand rupees." Mr *Kadar* sat down and replied, "Well suit yourself. I would have taken a total of ten thousand for the journey to Srinagar. My car can seat four of you so it would be only twenty five hundred a person. Moreover the ticket from Srinagar to Delhi is pretty cheap." This was a time when I had to take responsibility and make sure *Hrijan* reached home safely. So I stood up to speak for both of us, "Yes we also want a way out of this mess." My next query was directed to Thomas, "And how much does the ticket from Srinagar to New Delhi cost?" It was a meagre three thousand rupees. We had fifteen thousand rupees left with us. One look at the owner of the guest house and it appeared as if heavens had opened their gates and it was possible to make it to Delhi before Monday. *Hrijan* had a problem with this arrangement, "Newspaper is a luxury here in *Leh* and I haven't read the headlines for over a week now. But the last bulletin before our communication system collapsed announced a "state of emergency" in Srinagar. I bet that has not changed much in the last forty eight hours." Even Mr. *Kadar* looked startled. He knew *Hrijan* was right and roads to Srinagar might be choked-up. "Our valley is tormented by these recurring curfews you needn't worry about them." It seemed he had an alternative, "*Astitva* you, *Hrijan* and Thomas can come with me. Airport is on the outskirts and violence is confined to the more populous main city. I will take the payment once you reach the airport and not a penny before that." Money seemed to be the want of even the eleventh hour. The private airlines were minting money with extra flights scheduled for the next morning and so was this benevolent Mohammedan. He could not wait any longer and ordered in a concerned baritone, "Make sure our guests are satisfied with the last few days of their stay at our motel." He drove hurriedly and disappeared in to the night.

"Ha-ha... and you all were overwhelmed with my brother's generosity. He would never help his fellowmen leave alone you non-Kashmiris." The grin on *Bardaj*'s face had subsided and his forehead was outstretched in agony, "Even in this dreadful weather, when all hide in shallow shacks of their mud houses, he has to go back home, to Srinagar. His son leaves to study abroad tomorrow. When our father forced infidels out of our town *Kadar* marched next to him. This entitled him to be the patriarch of our clan." There was resentment in *Bardaj*'s voice. He shivered as he recalled those days of gore in Kashmir, "I was too young to lift a sword and kill my neighbour. My father did not consider it an excuse because even my classmates spearheaded this vicious attack on *Pundits* in Kashmir. Life never gave a second chance else I would go back to that day and kill more men than all my brothers combined." The words as they lurked out of his trembling lips were hollow. A man stood in front of us who would draw blood to prove to his family that his manhood had arrived. He was not tall but he was fair; his hair was black and his eyes were clear. Though he regretted not spilling blood, but his heart was thankful that his sword was not yet smeared. "Now if you will excuse me I will arrange for some food", and he walked downstairs so that *Tenzing* could continue.

"All of a sudden I was not looking at the road anymore. My bike crawled behind *Astitva*'s. There was no hurry. That hour when we sprawled on clouds my motorcycle did not move. It was the road that snaked beneath me. Sometimes it was the vista on the left which budged one arm length at a time. Rain stopped and we could see no rain Gods. Our gang marched in to those white billows stuffed with dew that dampened our clothes. *Hrijan's* face was sprinkled with freshness. His nose was still red but he looked restful now. Soroche manifested in varied forms amongst us throughout the trip from *Manali* to *Leh*, but it was not until today when we treaded the highest motorable road in the whole wide world that signs of psychological powerlessness surfaced. *Astitva* threw a half eaten apple down the valley and shouted at the top of his voice, "Here will be the fruitful tree of almighty *Astitva*." The sickness was contagious for on the next turn *Hrijan* threw a half eaten pear and shouted, "This spot shall mark the sinful tree of *Hrijan*." Quite naturally I should have joined my friends but the little bit of level-headedness remaining in me was busy appreciating the mountains that were slumbering in a thick white blanket of snow and cloud. If their trees were ever to grow green then it would be a vibrant display of natural pastels of fertility with a blank slate of snow in the background. To showcase this very abundance of determination in the youth I travelled all the way from West Bengal to *Leh*. However it seemingly became troublesome for us to maintain the same virility. This journey was to be measured in resolute chunks of breathtaking freedom only experienced by a traveller who has no destination. Such was the morale with we started on our bikes and every few miles evaded from us teaspoons of this resolve. Some of it was lost in convincing college students the importance of this trip and finally they agreed on the premises of an adventurous road trip. I have never travelled by an aeroplane. Of course I can afford it with the advent of aggressive private players in the aviation industry but I don't fancy myself as a bird. The road which we travel crosses *Khardung la Pass*. At an altitude of 18380 ft it is the closest you can get to the skies without flying. *Astitva* ran on the mountains with euphoric strides to go even higher than the signage that read "Highest Motorable Road in the World". I followed him to the steep and snow laden slopes. Once you reach the top and leave your motorcycle, each baby step consumes a lifetime of exasperation. My head got heavy and I used my hands to balance it in its place. My gait resembled a toper and I closed my eyes to stare at the blue heavens. Without a warning with snow that was old, brown and thinning, I was hit. I had always imagined snow to be downy. Somehow the snowballs were brittle to the bones. They tinged my ears and nose. *Astitva* was sitting down on a rock. His pseudo-trekking shoes had given up in this post blizzard trek. Our eyes searched for *Hrijan*. We hoped he was carrying the first aid kit. Our feet became numb and soon enough I fell on the snow. In a matter of seconds the vast scenery was somehow out of reach. The liberating Wind God blew radically to our rescue but neither of us nudged to its vigour. The valley down below had trenches several miles long but we could not peek in to them. We were not the first ones to arrive. Several trucks carrying supplies for our armed forces were parked on either side of the road. This very motorway is the lifeline that carries supplies to armed forces in *Siachin* Glacier. The tourists were busy with cameras, army men with security and children with their games. Understandably none of them could see two men lying helplessly with frozen feet. *Hrijan* was carrying coffee, one for each of us. He raised his glass and jeered, "Cheers!" before walking back to the other side of the road. *Hrijan* sat facing the temple of the mountain God. He needed rest as still half a day's travel remained for him to reach his friend. The coffee was steaming hot yet we gulped it down in a single mouthful. *Astitva* helped me get up and we took one step down at a time. I wanted to take off my wet shoes but under those weather conditions that would prove unpleasant. So we sat on the raised pavement next to the temple.

Fifteen minutes alone and *Hrijan* had already started off with his discourse, "War is indeed the mother of *Leh*, as is the case with many strategically located cities. Men built walls viewable from the Moon; they blew up mountains to carve roads and rails and even figured reasons of racial pedigree to divide a Nature which was never ours to begin with. Centuries ago it must have connected the southern Silk route bridging the gap between the Far East and Central Europe. Look at it now, the Chinese and Pakistanis vie for the control of this precious mountain pass to launch an attack on Indian sovereignty. The artery of cultural barter has mutated in to the vein of hostilities. But all hope is not wasted. Once the bad blood in my message reaches the heart of my friend he will purify my vagrantness."

People must have dismissed his disquisitions as they dispersed in to their assemblages of desultory divides. We followed his lead and strapped our helmets. The plan was to descend nonstop to the *Sumur* village in *Nubra* Valley. It was a good ninety kilometres to his friend's place. Nubra valley is also known as the valley of flowers and is nestled between the Ladakh and Karakoram ranges. The road was metalled and the only traffic was military trucks from opposite side. Somehow the worst of bad weather, jagged roads and frozen joints was behind us. Northern facade of the mountain was silent, quiet and a motorcyclist's paradise. Our eyes feasted upon the gorge that ran parallel to the road. The snow this side wasn't brown and was decorating the road on either side. After trading rubber with the gravel and tar of the highest motorable road in the world our motorcycles finally gave signs of weathering. The speed down-slope was without a doubt faster but the booming sound of the motorcycle had shrunk to a whimper. Probably it was the right time to fasten the nuts and bolts once again, within a blink of an eye *Astitva*'s motorcycle strayed and lost control. He managed to hit the tarmac on the mountain side while his helmet went off into the dale. Over one thousand kilometres withstanding swampy roads, tumbling boulders and none of us remembered to check the brake shoe. Only the front bakes were partly functional. Another fifty metres and his bike skid again. *Astitva* took to badgering, "The brake shoe is responding perfectly. Probably one of the wires was dislodged on the way." All three of us had grave expressions on our faces trying to figure out the problem. I exchanged bikes with *Astitva* and indeed the rear brake was not responding. *Hrijan* was silent and comparing his motorcycle with *Astitva*'s. "Can you make this journey with a single brake?" My question seemed inappropriate because the fact that hind shoes had worn out evidently suggested frequency of their use. *Hrijan* frisked his bag but the dismay on his face was unresolved. He sat in the centre of the road and stared into the oblivion on either side before disclosing the situation at hand, "*Astitva*. Your motorcycle is out of brake oil. We are not carrying any extra bottle for the road." *Astitva* was not disappointed, in fact he replied promptly, "Guess this is the end of the road for us. I will get the motorcycle towed back to *Leh.*" *Hrijan's* eyes were not on the road anymore. He stared at the skies and screamed in fury. His anger spiralled around an impasse. This journey had adjourned a doorway. *Astitva* sensed his disappointment, "Never mind, your friend would understand." *Hrijan* had shut his eyes by now but he was talking to us, "My friend who is staying in Nubra Valley has no clue of my arrival. He will be there just for three days." I suggested, "Considering the present circumstances we should complete the journey without *Astitva*. He can get the motorcycle fixed by the time we return from your friend's place." *Hrijan* stood up and stared me back into the eyes as he explained, "Rats desert a sinking ship. Do I look like a rat to you? We started off together and we will end this journey together." He took out the petrol canister, "Brake oil is an ether based fluid. Petrol should not work but it is worth giving a try."

My country has a government in exile. I will be contesting for college elections this year. This trip is to popularize our political party on campus. For the first time I felt a lot of myself coming in the way of national interest. Nascent inside me was a need to be recognised for my efforts. I enjoy limitless privileges in India. Leaving very little to complain about at a personal level and forcing me to wonder if *Hrijan* also had a message for me. Now that he knew the temporary technical setback we were all in agreement, "Definitely we can somehow manage to reach *Hunder* by nightfall. There must be a mechanic in that village." *Hrijan* mounted *Astitva's* motorcycle and turned it the other way, "No in fact we are going back to *Leh*. It is perilous to go any further. As fate has it my friend will have to wait." *Astitva* and *Hrijan* exchanged their motorcycles and we mounted our bikes. In a consoling voice I said, "Look on the brighter side, we sprawled on the highest motorway in the world on our motorcycles." *Hrijan* gave his helmet to *Astitva* and revved up the engine, "Look at the GPS navigator" It displayed 17,582 ft, "Several miles North-East of Khardung la, is Marsimik La. That is at an elevation of 18,314 ft and civilians are not allowed. So don't rejoice on trifle issues of altitude. I wasn't here to reach greater heights. Hundreds have walked this road before us; hundreds more will come. Nobody remembers our name and the feeling is mutual. Perhaps for some greater good I have to continue my nugatory travelogue."

〜☇〜

Family

Tenzing had been talking for over an hour now. Once the city of *Leh* was smothered in a black quilt cast by the witching hour, there was very little to do other than fear. Most of us trembling from head to toe; each heart was a pound heavier and thumping with frights of a flash flood gushing down the slope as we talked our hearts out. *Atiik* was shivering and he asked one of the brothers for an extra sweater. Most of our pullovers were wet so *Hrijan* had brought out his blanket on the roof. Rain does not visit us in the day, like a crouching tiger it waits till we fall asleep. It coverts in the night till our eyelids grow heavy. The fear had a smell. It was pungent to the extent of filth. If one paid attention he could locate the source of this odour. A walking source or shall we say a quivering source. "*Tenzing*, you are a very brave man. Some day you will lead your country to freedom." *Sahishnu* had vomit stains on his shirt which he did not wipe, "A dreadful night like this requires your ardour." Quite evidently personal hygiene was one of the key issues that were hit by an alarming fluctuation of altitude. He was about to enter his thirties and still grumbled like a whining schoolboy. The mop of hair that somehow survived premature ageing was oiled neatly to one side. He looked up to *Tenzing*. Now that his idol had lost all hope it was his obligation to come forth. Men with frail wits and fortitude need a woman's love to verve them up for an imminent occasion. They seek refuge in warm domestic nests. I call them good men. Great men rise from ashes and need no motivation other then the empathy for another man's apathy. So *Sahishnu* unknowingly put up a test for *Tenzing* that revealed a 'better' man.

He wiped his nose with a red handkerchief and recalled our first meeting, "First morning of the first day in the first week of August was very unwelcoming. As hosts these mountains do not entertain cragsmen in the rainy season. As history books articulate it whenever a handful of motivated men from our great *Maratha* clan desire to conquer the vast plains or steep hills of the North we land in between a rock and hard place. Centuries after the third battle of Panipat, not much has changed. It's been two days since I talked to my wife. Roads leading back home are choked. The sanctioned budget for our trip was twenty two thousand rupees; one stormy night and this is only half the price of each ticket that will take us back to civilization. The North Indians always cheat us. In the past it was the helpless *Nawabs* of *Oudh* who collaborated with some Arab invaders to conspire against us and now it is the *non-Marathi* speaking hapless tour operators who popularise cheap holidays in inescapable tragedies. Nothing much has changed." When we are sad our eyes moisten, when we worry our lips frown but it is only when all hope is lost that a man breaks into tears. *Sahishnu* evaded confrontations and with quivering lips requested, "Don't come near me. Words that enter my ears will not pacify me. My heart needs to divulge emotions of fear, hope and faith to placate me." So we gave him a patient hearing.

"The bus stop of *Manali* is always bustling with life. Tourists and explorers stop there midway in their travels. This meant we were not alone. Our bus was full of honeymooners and couples seeking a weekend retreat. To them the bad weather had little consequence; if possible they would stick to their beds for all eternity. All these couples had reached a destination and were pleased with the outcome of turbulent nights spent en route. Hence they were alighting from their buses and taxis. Our problem came with rucksacks. About several hundred backpackers cleaved to the crossbars of buses leaving early morning from *Manali* to *Leh*. Tickets were cheap and everyone had them. The conductor over drafted the receipts and later defended himself by giving us an option to travel all the way to *Keylong* standing. Somehow I always imagined foreigners to live in extravagant hotels, travel by air and eat lavishly but here they competed with us over the window seat of the rickety state tourism bus. French travellers were of course jaunting in giant families. The Spanish armada was missing its usual frivolity and our eyes were dying to see Indian faces travelling with us and then like a messiah came forward *Hrijan* with a smile on his face. "My name is *Hrijan*, I see your suitcases and they remind me of mine. You must be travelling to *Leh* by road." His Hindi had an inappropriate mixture of English words. But we agreed to his offer. As we followed him he was hard-selling the trip, "The driver lives in *Keylong* which is halfway between *Manali* and *Leh*. So he promised to take us there at a discounted rate." The taxi had ten seats. *Hrijan* helped us carry our luggage to the taxi. He exchanged a few words with the driver and ran off to get more customers. My elder brother for once mistook him for a taxi broker. Soon enough *Hrijan* filled the taxi with a mottled racial population. He took the seat next to the driver and had a basket sited against his feet. *Astitva* occupied the middle row with an ageing Italian couple. My elder brother contrary to his preference sat on the last bunk. He shared it with Thomas, the German. The Italian couple had a son who couldn't possibly be older than seven. His golden brown tresses covered his ears completely. Every time someone talked to him, he glanced at his mother for translation. As expected he was fluent only in his mother tongue. Moreover when we wanted to talk to his parents we had to speak in English very slowly. I wonder why is it that in my own country we lay utmost stress on dictions and punctuations of this foreign tongue, though I do not expect everyone to understand *Marathi* either.

Rohtang pass was not far from where we started our journey yet it wasn't before noon that we reached its chilly heights. A landslide conformed the highway into a one way street. For the first few hours trucks moved towards *Manali* and in the latter half of the day taxis could ply the converse way. *Astitva* got off to take a look around, "Where is the snow? I don't see any snow. There should be snow in *Rohtang* pass." We got off and everyone scattered on either side of the road. We took five steps in four directions and got lost in the fog. The driver said it wasn't just fog. He said it was the clouds that did not precipitate. Anyhow my brother got the blanket he needed to light a cigarette. The grass was green and our lips were blue. Past few months had been very taxing in terms of domestic harmony. In a bid to rekindle our brotherly love I planned this trip. My eyes searched for a smile on his face so that we could start our male bonding. *Shamasheel* always disapproved silence, "For once I let you take up responsibility for our trip and look where you have brought us, little brother." This was our lone time. He continued, "We can return to Mumbai tonight itself. Being this far away from civilization on our own won't do any good. It is our wives that quarrel. They ought to be out here." I love my wife and I love my brother. Somehow my sister-in-law doesn't endorse a common kitchen for the whole family of eight. Our mother was very desperate to find suitable girls and marry both of us. She would have never imagined this day. We never doubted her choice.

Bhaiya has always taken refuge in nature photography. I prayed *Leh* would help him relax. And once I broke the news to him, he would have plenty of time to reason it out with me. What else would he do in the alien town of *Leh*? Antagonistic heights of *Rohtang* did not qualify as the apt place for such a conversation. Moreover our back pockets were wet with stains of dew, nonetheless he lit the first few fumes and I objected because my brother always maintained he was a social smoker. "What exactly is a social smoker?" He would ask. Inevitably every time we were to nail a discussion on chain smoking of lone men, he would be joined by another chain smoker. This time he bonded with a foreigner. Thomas had two hands; one of them was always preoccupied with a German M43 style field cap. It was in military green colour and was rarely marketed after 1976. With the other he approached my brother, "Do you have a light?" He sat right in between us. I walked back to the taxi. The view from the window was murky, restricted and disagreeable. While many a tourists found it hard to come to terms with the increasing height, thinning air and grubbing ground my brother smoked his lungs out. Inside the taxi I talked to the aged woman. She asked me to whisk out an apple from the basket under the front seat. The charming lady from *Kokhsar* owned orchids of tangy green apples in *Manali*. Once every two or three months she tends to the fruit bearing trees.

Suddenly everyone rushed to their cars. Our driver pressed on the accelerator and honked at our fellow travellers. People were running with cramped joints on the chilly hills of *Manali*. The gates were never closed and as we climbed the slope our taxi got heavier. Nobody knew how long the army would keep the passage open. Everyone wanted to be the first one to exit. As the car picked up speed, our ride got bumpier. Most of the road had been washed away. It was no more a two lane highway rather a by lane along a mountain side resort. *Hrijan* turned around and stared at my hands, "Would you happen to have another one of those apples, a green apple!" He sighed, although apple is not an exquisite fruit in India but the tartly juice of this special variety that grows in *Himachal* was visibly wobbling *Hrijan's* taste buds. The expression on his face was not of gluttony, it was a thrilling mixture of appreciation for the sheer beauty that was commanded by nature and her fruits, so the kind lady offered him an apple. In fact she offered everyone in the car an apple. She smiled while handing one to the oblivious Italian lad, "This is the first plucking for our own domestic use. My grandnephew loves them." Without a warning and with several jerks our car screeched to a halt. The tires rolled, but as they were smudged in mud they did not move an inch. Again with a thud the car jerked. This time it wasn't the brake. Boulders were tumbling from the greased mountains which did not take to our presence pleasantly.

Burrrrhhhh... was the noise that zipped past us. Louder was his message, "Our friend is stuck with his motorcycle back there. The crag may crush him any moment. Help us pull him out." And he went straight ahead, way beyond the muddy patch of road. We were in the back seat. The rear window had a critical vantage view. Three motorcyclists were furiously throttling their bikes but the rear tires stuck to the mud. With each attempt they sank deeper and deeper. My brother suggested that we got out. *Astitva* insisted on pulling the motorcycles with a rope fastened to our taxi and Thomas articulated his scepticism, "This car cannot carry its own weight leave alone dragging those motorcycles." Hearing this most men in the car shuddered and the women froze their expression to exclaim a chest pain but I could feel the conjuring courage. Miracle was already out there right behind us on the road. God helps man one step at a time and one man at a time. *Hrijan* lifted the hind wheel of the blue motorcycle and pushed it across the slippery road. The rider directed from the front wheel and by the time we finished an argument in the car one motorcycle was already on steadier grounds. The Italian man was furious, "You stupid driver. Save our souls first, no need to help them. Stop staring and press on the throttle." His wife was equally livid, "We have a baby in this car. Can't you see we are a priority?" The second bike had an overloaded saddle. It took three monstrous men with hurting arms to lift it off the ground. *Hrijan* walked towards them and asked each one to carry one of the rucksacks containing the camping gear. Again he took the hind wheel and smiled at the rider in front, "That ought to speed up the rescue mission." As soon as the last motorcycle was carried to safety, the road behind us gave way to a cleft. It was our turn and though the driver was burning the wheels it hardly nudged the car. We all exited the vehicle. It was the driver and his car against the road. Thomas unfastened his bag from the taxi and in the process dislodged all other bags as well. Eight of us clinging to solid ground with one hand and our baggage in the other were crying for help. The driver was still fighting, only now he had all the four motorcyclists helping him. They placed stones under both the rear wheels. The tires now had solid ground to tread upon. Driver started from the first gear. After every rotation *Hrijan* and his new found friends shifted the stone further. The driver had to press the throttle and then apply the brakes almost immediately to keep proceeding. At the far end was another jam of vehicles. Some four-wheelers waited for us to clear the path while others fled at the site of a caving road. Twenty six minutes and four aching spines later we crossed the precarious road. An army man was waiting to greet us. He shoved past my brother and interrogated the driver. Most of us would have returned if the remaining journey proffered a similar quest, however there wasn't much choice. The road behind us had fallen. The only escape was the road ahead and so we loaded our luggage again onto the taxi.

Meanwhile *Hrijan* had a chat with one of the motorcyclists. Four interstate cruiser motorcycles, painted in red, yellow, blue and white, lined the road in front of us. Two of them had a female pillion rider. All six riders were wearing multicoloured arm bands. *Hrijan* introduced his new friend, "Everyone this is *Tenzing*. *Tenzing* meet everyone." *Tenzing* smiled when we greeted him. His red nose contrasted perfectly with tanned cheeks. The road had apparently taken a toll on his attractive features. Very enthusiastically he shook our hands. Now the arm band was vivid. It was a landscape composition with the Sun rising from behind a mountain painted in yellow radiance and alternating red-blue rays diverging in a rectangular pattern. We still had a long way before we could reach *Keylong* so we took off. *Tenzing* and his gang were busy with their motorcycles. Either they were repairing it or preparing it. No matter which way you prefer it they were indeed very busy, so we took the lead. The road ahead was a sharp descend from the heights of *Rohtang*. A wicked landscape was on display. My elder brother couldn't get his finger away from the shutter. The rain had stopped and even the Sun paid a visit. The hills were not even green. The road was void of any restaurants or motels. Moreover as a consequence of the landslide we were the only travellers.

Gradually the journey had lost its adventure quotient. The driver looked weary. My brother had kept the DSLR away. Thomas had dozed off. His last words complained about the smoothness of this journey, "We might as well flock on the living room couch. Oh this is so great, an off-road adventure with hardly any room to tussle my arm." No matter how uncomfortably but he indeed fell asleep on *Astitva*'s shoulder. Time and again *Hrijan* would turn around. He seemed pretty comfortable besides the driver but something was bothering him. At first I considered it my imagination but surely something was cooking between *Hrijan* and Thomas. So when my brother requested to exchange seats with *Hrijan* I got to observe him ever more closely. The driver asked us to wait till *Kokhsar* to exchange seats. The old lady added very politely, "This is where I get off. We have been travelling all day. You all must be awfully tired." Our taxi halted next to a bridge and she got off. "It may not be much but I would like to invite all of you for a cup of tea at my house." The driver looked more annoyed than pleased although he was in dire need of a fresh cuppa. Thomas had his reservation about the water used for making the tea. Anyhow most of us finally gave into the temptation of hot tea and biscuits. Her house wasn't far away from the highway so we walked. The lady had a lot to tell us about her dwelling. "This is the coldest place in *Lahaul* and we offer home stay for some tourists. At my age, it becomes terribly monotonous to live all by myself. In fact I think we do have some guests staying in the out-house this week." We sat in her garden while she called forth her guests. The girl behind her was carrying a kettle. A splendid girl I must say. I was reminded of my sweet wife. This trip served the dual purpose of facilitating some brotherly bonding and also escaping domestic responsibility. It's been only three days and I have started missing the ladies of my house. This young girl was from Jordan. She had blue-green eyes and helped the elderly lady in setting up a comfy evening tea. Soon we were joined by the little girl's family. Her father was evidently fed on goats and cows all his life while the mother seemed to have developed a permanent baby bump. Her sisters were busy adjusting the earphones of their portable music players and their little brother had gone up the hill with his uncle. Our stay was prolonged by *Hrijan's* absence. Apparently he had disappeared with his cup. He had a very pleasant companion and indeed we did not expect him to return anytime soon. All this family time was making me desperate to talk to my wife and daughter. My elder brother was one step ahead and he had already made the call. Ironically enough even his daughter was out shopping with her boyfriend. Suddenly the garden had three worrying fathers and a very debatable topic. It seemed Jordanians had quite similar fears and their brawny physique did little to ward off the teenage tantrums. The Italian couple was yet to face such a episode. In many ways they were still experiencing the first few engaging years of marriage. Thomas stood up after we emptied the kind lady's teakettles. Though she insisted but we asked her not to accompany us back to the taxi as it was getting dark. It was again a short walk across the bridge to the cramped spaces of our taxi. *Hrijan* was standing next to the car and shouted from the other side of the road, "What took you all so long?" He kissed the Jordanian muscleman's daughter goodbye and hopped onto the last seat. "I have been waiting here for ages. *Shamasheel* you get to sit in the front now. Thomas and I have a lot to talk about." And that was the last we spoke of the kind orchard woman.

As we drove nearer to his hometown the driver got excited, "*Hrijan* sir, I see your hair is wet. Did you get real close to the drool worthy river?" *Hrijan* never needed any provocation to share with us his observations. Though I hadn't paid much attention initially but now even I took notice. Thomas initiated the bantering, "Did you get her name and number?" *Hrijan* looked puzzled and *Astitva* came to his rescue, "He made most out of the hour. What good is a number? We won't be visiting them again." Even the Italian lady joined our persiflage, "*Hrijan* If I may add, the two of you make a very adorable couple. The reflection of her milky complexion is still visible in your green eyes." *Hrijan* turned away to face the window but his embarrassment was expressed in shades of red and the toddler, sitting in the middle row, pointed a finger at his cheeks as he blushed. Almost everyone beamed at the thought of teenage romance blossoming on the road and along the banks. Thomas hinted towards an exciting week in *Leh* with all the tourists from exotic cities of the world unexpectedly facing *Hrijan's* romantic advances. *Bhaiya* calmed everyone from the front seat and extended his arm to shake hands with *Hrijan*, "Only the workaholics of New Delhi know how to kindle love at first sight. You are even snappier than these foreigners." The ride got bumpier back in the boot. Maybe the rear suspensions had worn out thanks to the grump road. The lovely jostles of puppy love excited our driver and his buggy. Soon the jesting stopped and I was pleased to see my brother sleep contentedly besides the driver. However the silent Italian man had a problem with that. He would pinch or shove my brother every now and then. Finally he turned around and complained to me, "Mr. *Sahishnu* would you be kind enough to tell your brother not to fall asleep next to the driver." Intruding words of this gentleman needed a tough talk. We had been travelling all day. Our bottoms had been gyrating with every puddle long the road and now that my brother finally had a cushioned headrest this intruder wouldn't let him get some shut eye. I folded my sleeves as to intimidate him but my brother's smoke-buddy was keen to support the Italian, "You don't need to take it as a personal attack on your brother, calm down." *Astitva* added that once the front passenger sleeps it is that much more probable that our dear driver will also fall asleep. Someone suggested that if my brother wants to sleep he can do that at the back. Thirty five years have gone by and my brother has never complained about a rough patch on the journey. Even today when these strangers would request him to change the seats he would agree, in spite of having a lumber spondylosis. *Hrijan* found both the issues to be of genuine concern. He glanced at my brother who was ignorant to our debate. He needed the rest.

And then suddenly with a flush of embarrassment *Hrijan* proposed, "Mr. Driver sir, how about I tell you the story of a Jordanian lass and a river?" He took out a camera. Everyone got their turn to look at the pictures taken in the eventide. *Hrijan* rested his feet on the opposite plank and closed his eyes. In a dreamy voice he addressed the girl from Jordan, "Don't tell me your name. I won't be able to forget it ever. Rather let me entitle you to all the agnomens that try to elucidate your ubiquity. Let this perpetual moment on the river bank by the mountain side be your appellation for the rest of my life. Henceforth I will refer to you in the numbing chilliness of my evenings. My eyes will trace your bearing in every meandering river. Your scents will forever fall on me when I lie on the wet mountain grass. If you tell me your name today, you will cease to exist as an enticement unlike this inviting brook." He muffled in his dream to recount the girl's reply, "*Vitasta*, I will give you a name to rummage me by. It is the name of this river beside whose banks we embrace each other. Can't you see how cold it is? Come closer, you still have miles to go." *Hrijan* had awakened the lover in each one of us. Staring back through the misty windows of our car he recalled the sunset, "It all began with her nose that tickled away the frothing intimidation from my neck, much like the inviting splashes of the river. When I opened my eyes to unclasp her torso as we rolled on the moist grass the river gurgled past the rocks twisting and turning with us. The same lips that warmed my lobes had a balmy effect as they brushed my tussling guts. She said, "Even the river has a tepid breath once you embrace its depth." The Italian lady was engulfed in the lard of love, "Too bad it did not last long young man." *Hrijan* wiped a few tears as he turned around to answer the lady, "*Vitasta* is born every moment in the hot water springs of *Verinag*. She is pure and has no memory. When we crossed that bridge, we left it forever so that it may flow down all the way to Pakistan." *Astitva* interrupted to tell him that we were not talking about the river anymore, but he continued to speak in his stupor, "She exchanges breaths with everyone who walks beside her. Their story intermingles often beyond these hills. And they shall never dip in the same waters again for such is the nature of *Vitasta* she abodes in our heart snugly.

"What? What did I miss? Have we reached Leh already?" My brother sounded sluggish as he startled us somnolently.

I guess we all have our very own Vitasta and we miss her very much."

Quietness spoke aloud for the next ten minutes, betraying that silence was our desolation. Everyone was fighting with his demon. Everyone was lurking in memories of years gone by and tears that did not bleed. Just like every story had a villain it also had a *Vitasta*, the nimble recluse which brushed our souls once and moved on. We all cried because we could not live those moments again and we cried a little more because it pleasured us to know that she still dwelled inside of us. *Shamasheel* was the first one to return from the reverie as he wiped off tears from his brother's face. And *Sahishnu* smiled back at the touch of motherly love. He was never an opportunist but nobody could seize that moment from him and he confessed, "*Bhaiya*, my wife wants me to lure you out all the way to *Leh* and then like a stalking lion unleash the arsenal of words that would pierce your heart." *Sahishnu* and *Shamasheel* were embracing each other from the shoulders. "However the fabric that holds us brothers together will survive the test of time." They did not have much time. That night was all they had. *Sahishnu* ended his pretentious brave demeanour. He shrunk into his brother's warm embrace. For that hour was long enough to end all longing of flesh and faith. Lucky are those who end their journey together. If god made one bleak he made sure the elder was caring enough to encase all around. With responsibility came sensibility. *Shamasheel* strained from crying. He had better things to do. He went downstairs to get his mobile phone and find the immaculate inclination and alleviation for mobile service reception. The night was long and the brothers had it all to themselves. They were finally at peace.

In his brother's absence *Sahishnu* couldn't resist to tell us another truth, "I am going to stop pretending to be brave. I am scared to die here on this mountain thousands of kilometres away from my wife and children." His voice became agonised as he held *Tenzing* from the cloak, "Meet my childhood hero. These days he is too busy playing my caretaker. The eve of 3rd August, when you met us in the hosiery shop it was I who needed an excuse. You, Thomas, *Astitva* and *Hrijan* would have anyhow taken your motorcycles to the highest road in the world but I did not want to lose my brother for your petty road trip. *Shamasheel* never even found out about your little expedition. I am to be blamed for my brother's cowardice and aloofness." *Tenzing* had mentioned it to us while having dinner the other night. He saw *Sahishnu* and *Shamasheel* buy T-shirts from a local hosiery shop with a slogan that popularised road trips to *Khardung la*. At numerous occasions *Shamasheel* had shown interest to partake an adventure with us so it was quite natural for us to invite him. Unfortunately it always brought forth the poundage of responsibilities that weigh down the adventurer inside *Shamasheel*. *Sahishnu* made an honest attempt to testify for his brother's courage but *Shamasheel* was not listening. He was still downstairs searching for his mobile phone. And I guess these words addressed the other hero amongst us, the one whose motorcycle was flagged red, yellow and blue. Desperation had creaked its way into *Sahishnu's* words. *Tenzing* needed to be stronger. His mates had abandoned him in the eleventh hour. When the dreary accept their ill-fate it is the duty of the brave to guide them. *Tenzing* stared depressingly at the empty seat on his motorcycle which was parked all alone. He had lost the right to lead and the riders from Bengal were returning without him.

Keylong To Leh

I still did not know the dispute which divided *Tenzing* and his biker gang. Like most doyens he took upon the task of leading his friends on this road trip religiously. However the true motive of this trip was political as we found out in *Keylong*.

We reached the city located midway between *Leh* and *Manali* at eight in the night. The settlement was void of any commotion. Our driver parked the car and his family hogged us. They offered us beds in their small house at concessional rates. The Italian couple retired in one of the tacky student hostels. Everyone was tired and the thought of warm, cosy bed sheets was irresistible. *Hrijan* made a trunk call to his family in Delhi. Thomas was going through the last few days' account in *Hrijan's* journal. Both of them had grown immensely fond of each other. They used to sign the journal every night. All of us had packed our luggage neatly, for our journey tomorrow would begin even before day break. The manager of the small guest house where we put up took the payment up-front. It was around ten in the night and *Hrijan* returned with steaming hot food. He took a plateful of vegetables to the loggia. Thomas accompanied him. The rain had stopped but it was still freezing out there and they snuggled into a blanket. The bellboy knocked on our door. He held out his right hand, "Sir your friend left in a hurry and there was considerable change left. This is the balance. Would you like anything else?" The two of them had their gaze fixed at the stars of the rain laundered sky. It wouldn't hurt their pockets much if I asked them to pay for my beer; even better they would never know so I ordered a pint and the night passed out quietly. The following morning my worst nightmare confronted me. There were two tickets on the table next to the bed. I assumed Thomas must have bought *Hrijan* and my ticket along with his own. My mobile phone was used as a paper weight. Five hundred rupees and a letter lay under it along with the tickets. *Hrijan* had deserted me and the letter did little to explain it. I read it to the entire group in the wee hours of 8th August standing on the stock pile of firewood beside the bonfire.

"Dear *Astitva*,

Would you ever believe that it took me twenty three years to prepare for the trip of my life? Though it sounds farfetched but such is the truth. The little things, we abide by must make way for the bigger things. What? Why? How? The fine print of moral code was never as subjective as it is today. We must answer these questions for ourselves. We can't let anyone or any society dictate those to us on the pretext of religion, region, or colour. If you are to continue this journey then it must be out of free will. We offer you a choice. Take a closer look at the tickets. One will take you back home to Delhi where your wife awaits and the other is a call from my friend who is holidaying in *Nubra* Valley beyond *Leh*.

Astitva you are a good man and we enjoy your company, however Thomas and I had planned this trip together even before you were invited by chance."

I hadn't finished reading *Hrijan's* disposition when *Atiik* interrupted, "I very well understand the emotions that bring forth this letter. Any sensible man would have liked to have a word with *Hrijan* on that occasion." He glanced at *Hrijan* in dismay, "You should have never disappeared. If only you would have discussed with *Astitva* the peculiar pretext of this trip in front of your brother." Fire always forges the strongest and strangest of bonds. As the wood burnt with a popping sound and *Atiik* scolded *Hrijan* I learnt the reason to be here. Advising a twenty three year old is easy because you don't expect him to listen or act upon your words. All you expect is that he makes mistakes and learns from them. The only obligation we have as predecessors is, to make sure that they own up to their mistakes. My marriage might have been a mistake but not making peace with my wife was a transgression of the solemn bond that unifies us. Troubled by fears of death and the ultimate judgement our heart recounts endless lives that we constituted. I could only thank *Hrijan* but *Atiik* wouldn't understand the mysterious ways in which god works, so instead I continued finishing the last lines of the letter,

"*Tenzing* reached *Keylong* at the stroke of midnight. He represents the Students Freedom Movement of Tibet. My friend in Nubra Valley would appreciate this firsthand experience with unproven voyagers of his government in exile. No wonder his gang had two empty pillion seats. Meet us at old *Leh* bus stop. We will wait till the last bus arrives. Whatever be your decision we are sure you will understand. Complete this road trip for the right reasons."

Five days before the flood, after reading this letter on a cold night in *Keylong* all alone in the lavish room of the guest house I realized that *Hrijan* might not be as violent and as infamous as his elder brother but he is equally rogue. Baby-sitting a twenty something man is a painstaking job. There were still two hours for the bus to leave and I went back to sleep. People on the roof were divided in their opinion. *Shamasheel* was excited to know that I took the plunge into untested waters as an adventurer while Thomas was disappointed as he would not get the much deserved lone time with *Hrijan*. *Atiik* denounced his decision, "God bless. Allah offered you respite from this dreadful fate, only if you would have accepted the other ticket *Astitva*." *Tenzing* acknowledged my courage and offered his friendship, "Had we known about your intentions we would have arranged for an extra motorcycle. It would have been nice to have your company on the dusty tracts that connect *Keylong* to *Leh*." My ears longed to hear *Hrijan's* opinion but he did not share my enthusiasm instead very reluctantly he handed over the stage to Thomas, who walked across the floor to sit next to *Hrijan*.

Graveness of an impending fate transmuted into animation as Thomas began his epilogue, "Most Indian motorcycles are cheap copies of their European and American cousins sans the horse power churning engines. Astonishingly I have grown fond of the absurdly unique road etiquettes of this country. If I were to ever describe *Hrijan* in one word it would have to be infectious. After finishing my key note at the conference in Delhi on 29th July, I decided to take a week off. This whole week my cargos haven't been washed. As if I have just one pair to live by. Ninety litres of strategic space in my backpack is overflowing with disposable razors, extra pair of slippers, a sleeping bag and my tickets, yet somehow this trip qualifies for a backpacking adventure. His gait is unlike any traveller that I have ever seen. With a distinctive brown sling bag he roams the towns hoping to meet only those people who are receptive to his love. At my first glance on his juvenile romance with the freshly melted waters of *Beas* river I was shocked. But every time he sprang out he had a bigger smile on his face. Very few of us are chosen children of destiny. *Hrijan* is loved by nature and he knows it. Mother Nature seeks out excuses to caress him and he responds with a threadbare soul. We were holding hands when he taught me the first lesson of backpacking and thus began the undraping of my anima very early that morning.

Eight travellers, four motorcycles, two prima donnas and one road, *Leh* couldn't get any more exciting. One girl rode with her brother while the other with her boyfriend. One could tell the difference upon measuring the room for air to pass between the pillion and the rider. The first few hours were covered rather hurriedly. We wanted to reach *Darcha* and witness the sunrise from the sedimentary bed of its dried up seasonal streams. *Tenzing* set the pace for us in his overloaded highway cruiser. Overtaking was forbidden so we crawled like a centipede treading to the bottom of the mountain. These mountains have a rather inconvenient network of roads. Each kilometre is covered in a dog year and then we descend with great caution only to rise again for the next mountain pass. There were five such passes on the road from *Manali* to *Leh*. We alternatively stopped at three of them. Sometimes to capture nature's kaleidoscope in our cameras and sometimes to relieve us of browbeaten bladders.

An emerald lake at *Baralacha La* was one such stop. The sparkling water got a chirpy reception from the two girls. This also gave me plenty of time to observe the bands on our arms. They bore a flag representing the country sheltered by Snow-capped Mountains. The original six tribes unite in the form of six red rays emanating the sky. These mountains are protected by two deities one red and the other blue, hence the alternate band of colours in the flag. Ever ushering Sun in the centre sprinkled upon the subjects a light of wisdom in the same token to all. A pair of mythical snow lions with graphically animated features symbolizes the complete victory over self. Beckoning bicoloured jewels clasped by these lions spoke for the ten divine virtuous actions and sixteen human morals. The Amaranthine teachings of Gautama Buddha adorn this nation with a golden radiance bordering the flag. These youths on their oil guzzling motorcycles wanted a free Roof for the World. *Tenzing* laid stress on spending majority of the time on the road. Probably he was the only one who looked forward to the destination. None of these stops were longer than ten minutes. From where *Tenzing* saw it he would have to wait that much longer for Tibet's freedom. Beyond this point a race ensued between spouses.

According to legend Chandra, daughter of the Moon God married Bhaga, son of the Sun god in a celestial ceremony atop this very mountain. They ran in opposite directions much like the rivers christened after them which originate at the emerald lake and venture outwards on separate paths. I rode with *Tenzing* in a bid to outdo *Hrijan*, who was at the back of the pack. For the first time in my life I discovered true wilderness. We were out in the dusty *Moore* Plains which were yet to be stamped with gravel and tar. Rocky hills on either side did little to cool the afternoon sun. For the hundredth time I used the word boundless to describe our possibilities. The beeline had been broken and four motorcycles were neck to neck. Whenever someone drove fast enough to reach the front of the pack, birds of scrounge would gather above us to mimic our skein. I was the only one who glared at the skies. Others were too busy attempting to breathe in the cloud of dust that followed us. The girls covered their faces with shawls and all the pillions crouched behind the rider. *Hrijan* improvised his multicoloured muffler into a taglemust. As we slowed down I signalled at him to remove his goggles but he did not respond. He had removed his helmet and I was begging for a glimpse of his crystalline eyes. Even with all of his face under the cheche he attracted me and I longed for his touch. For several hours he sat very still on that bike probably smiling under the veil and for the longest time I recalled our long conversations over the internet. I wondered how charmingly he would have repeated those words piercing my heart with his wanton smile. So far we had to share our room with *Astitva*. This left us with only a few hours of privacy when he would be fast asleep. Even in those secret dialogues he thanked me for accompanying him. Several months ago, during our initial conversations on Skype I would have never expected that this twenty something brown skinned boy from India would one day teach me the art of inspiration. Often he reminds me that he is not sexually attracted to me but almost instantly he adds that he couldn't imagine somebody else to spend his life with. My visor was getting hazy and I could not wipe off my tears so I stared through the foggy desert at the symbol of freedom on his arm. *Hrijan* walked away from his house, he loved people he met on the journey and remembered to not make any promises. He was free and if god forbid we die this very night, I am sure he would let me fall in his arms one last time."

We witnessed their first kiss of diffidence. Those seven days of adventure had subdued the flame of passion and made way for a halcyon moment of assertion. Of course not all ten of us accepted this union. Then again most of us did not matter to the couple. They would have happily drowned in the flood that night embracing each other as they walked into the afterlife. Their glued lips provoked a mixture of fluids from my mouth as well and I had to turn around so as to not face them. But everyone else was lurking with venom filled prose at the sight of quintessential lovers. I walked downstairs before the old man could outcast them as by-products of westernization; before the brothers from Mysore could condemn them to be yields of un-Islamic education; or even before *Sahishnu* could incorporate the indecent act of homosexuality in his dictionary of possibilities. I walked downstairs where another couple was hugging each other. Their children were asleep and they needed reassurance of a life after this night and what better remedy than the lips of your spouse to tell you of hope. Maybe I wasn't disgusted by the lip-lock upstairs all I wanted was to spend this moment in the same act with my partner. A partner who has forgotten me much like the river *Chandra* whose lover *Bhaga* chose to walk away. My dear wife worked as a nurse in a big government hospital. She had been the sole bread winner for several years now. Even after repeated endoscopies and ultrasounds we couldn't conceive a child. This was one of my principle arguments when I filed for divorce. Our families were very much aware of the strained marital chords yet they longed us to stick together for safeguarding the honour of both the families. She had been living in her father's house for past sixteen months and I had not written a single letter. In bygone years when we double shifted to make ends meet I used to look for excuses to show up in the hospital where she worked but all those sweet nothings had banished from our relationship. We hadn't exchanged a single syllable of romance in the years that followed my dismissal from service. Early that morning we had informed *Hrijan's* brother of our predicament. Despite the fact that it was my turn to make the call, I couldn't remember her phone number. My only wish that night was to somehow hear her voice. I cursed the day I deleted her name from my friend list. I missed a lot of Thomas' account in my contemplation. By the time I returned to the roof he was explaining *Shamasheel* the mechanics of navigating an inflatable kayak. This surprised me because Thomas was scared of water. He agreed to accompany *Hrijan* on the white water raft after hours of persuasion. In fact I do remember the night of 2nd August when they came to receive me at the old *Leh* bust stop on their newly rented motorcycles. Thomas was hugely dissatisfied with the meagre sixteen horses powering his bike, "Back home in Germany I own a BMW R1200 that offers 61N-m of raw cruising power. Now look at the best selling motorcycle of your country. I might as well ride a bicycle." He even carried pictures of his fancy collection of two wheelers. He could talk about motorcycles for days and about road-trips for weeks, but little did we know that this journey of ours will be remembered for generations to come.

After finishing our dinner we toured the little town of *Leh* in search of that ideal pad to put our bags. This was also the first time when I witnessed Thomas and *Hrijan* squabble like a peevish couple in post honeymoon phase. The subject matter was a fancy bathroom. Thomas sat with me in the lobby as *Hrijan* negotiated ineffectively with the hotel manager. He brought a brochure, "It is the off-season and they will offer us a double room for two thousand. The same room sells for Seven thousand usually." Thomas got up to leave, "This is way too much for a fancy bathroom." I followed them as they quarrelled through the lobby and walked across the patio. Thomas was getting irritated now, "We would have been in bed by now if you would have agreed to spend the night in a backpacker hostel." *Hrijan* overreacted to this accusation, "Why is it always about bed with you guys? Sometimes accommodation is also about safety and hygiene." Thomas favoured the cheap stand alone room for rent near the old bus stop, "It had huge floor area, a pink coloured double bed and the owner even offered an additional mattress for *Astitva* at no extra cost. What else do you want for two hundred rupees?" *Hrijan* stopped at the sight of the grandest hotel in town market. I waited at the reception while the two of them visited several rooms. When they returned Thomas was full of praises, "I love the mauve drapes on the second floor. Did you fancy the picturesque panorama of the hills from the first floor balcony? And they also offer room service." The expression on *Hrijan's* face was miffed, "It's too fancy. We just need a bed and a bathroom." So next we went to a budget motel up the same road. The gate keeper was the bell boy as well as the receptionist and also the owner and the landlord. Only a single room was available and this triggered a smile on *Hrijan's* face. This room has all the necessities and no shenanigans to overcharge us. Thomas had serious concerns, "You cannot be serious. All three of us on that single bed. I wouldn't check-in even if the queen shared it with me." So we continued our search for the perfect room in this small town. Three hotels later I decided to camp on the road. We had been walking for over two hours yet they were not able to reach an agreement. Thomas was agitated by the peculiar choices *Hrijan* made. He seriously considered splitting up and spending the night in a separate hotel. *Hrijan* was in a habit of taking us for granted and when Thomas confronted us with his solution *Hrijan* considered it a betrayal. Thomas explained, "Consider this, I go back to the first room we visited today and you continue this aimless search of yours. After spending the night in a beautiful, affordable and spacious room I meet you early tomorrow morning. Hopefully by then you would get tired of roaming the empty streets." We sat on the pavement for some time. Thomas hinted at the lights visible on either side of the road, "There are at least a hundred modernised rooms available down that street and we have visited all of them. You would give my most finical girlfriend a run for her money." "Modernised? I think you mean Westernized!" *Hrijan* screamed furiously at the empty street, "There was no water in the god forsaken toilet you paper-wiper." Many tourists peeped out of their first floor windows and I suppose they were all Westerners. As the last of the windows shut again tensions dissolved and both of them sat their laughing at other's misery. As they rolled down the street jesting each other a new character beheld us. Very small in stature and very red in complexion, we didn't stop rolling even at his feet. In a thick Kashmiri accent he asked, "Did anyone of you gentlemen just address my foreign guests on the basis of their unique absence of hygiene?" *Hrijan* stood up clumsily and Thomas was still laughing.

The stranger hid a smile under his dyed beard and he spoke patiently,

"You are on the wrong street" he swept his eyes about the main road and stooped at the sight of a German, "with inappropriate companions."

I interrupted apologetically, "We were just scooting. You need not bother yourself over something so small and so true." Our joke hadn't even ceased being funny and he was joined by three more men. Apparently they worked for him. Thomas understood the implications of our lingering any longer and pulled *Hrijan* away, "Well I guess we better leave." The apparently rich gentleman seemed to be a man of means. He told *Hrijan* looking straight into his eyes, "It is about time you left. I have already arranged for the car. These men will take you to my personal guest rooms. Only once in a blue moon do we get to meet boys who are yet to grow up." The three employees carried our luggage into a van. The old man accompanied us to the car. He held out his hand and introduced himself, "My name is *Kadar*. I am growing fond of you, young man. You remind me of my lost youth." *Kadar* had deep grey dreamy eyes filled with regrets. *Hrijan* did not agree with him, "Youth is never lost, it matures into wisdom." Unruffled *Kadar* replied, "Come here tomorrow first thing in the morning. We will talk of how an entire lifetime can be wasted." Thomas interrupted their conversation; He reminded *Hrijan* of the rafting tickets they had booked for the next day. *Hrijan* ignored Thomas and agreed to Mr. *Kadar*'s offer, "Good night, sleep now or you shall be late for *Fajr* tomorrow. I will meet you after the prayers." And the two of them bowed with their eyes.

The driver was a migrant from Tibet. He drove us through the twirling streets. Mr. *Kadar*'s guest house was considerably away from the main market. His neighbours had barns on either side of his guesthouse. The car stopped in front of the building with the biggest keystone. The driver brought out a gasoline cylinder from the trunk of the van and hurriedly placed it at the door mat. We followed him into the "*Khan's Inn*" when he suddenly turned around and shrieked in enragement. He signalled us to wait outside and rang the bell. Once we crossed the blind turn on the street he explained, "Actually sir, this guest house is partly owned by Mr. *Kadar* and partly by his third step mother. Instead of selling the house and dividing the money they decided to bifurcate the building. You were entering the wrong side. Mr. *Kadar* owns the backside of the house." Thomas found it rather suspicious and enquired, "If that is so why did you leave the cylinder on the door?" A very diplomatic answer awaited us, "Sir, I serve the house, the family and the monetary benefits I receive are not bound by lines drawn between dwellers of this house." This unavoidably led to the next question, "What if someday you have to make a choice?"

We reached the reception. A ghastly fair man was sleeping on the bench opposite the gate. The driver woke him up and looked back to address us, "Sir, I am not good at politics. I have been forced to leave my homeland by oppressors from the Far East. I cannot afford to tiff either of them so the best option in this hypotherical situation would be to find another job." He left us with the sleepy caretaker.

"Greetings my dear friends, I am *Bardaj*," he rubbed his eyes to get a clear idea of how many rooms would be required and enquired in a dopey tone, "You must be special guests of *Kadar*. He is my elder brother." To Thomas' displeasure *Hrijan* began his usual negotiation, "We would like the most affordable room here to spend the night." It took a while for our drowsy host to scroll his register. He asked us to sign in the register and offered a single key. We followed him up to the third floor and he showed us the last room on the aisle that led to the balcony. Dropping our bags on the bed he requested, "Give me an hour as I have to look for the extra mattress." To this Thomas objected, "That won't be necessary. I want a separate room. This room is too small for three men to stay." *Hrijan* signalled Thomas through the corners of his eyes to come outside. Gradually they were evolving into a degenerate quarrelsome couple. Thomas seemed genuinely concerned about the floor area. In fact the receptionist told us that all rooms on the top floor were smaller in order to make room for the conference hall. *Hrijan* was angry, "So now you don't want to spend the night with me. Isn't the view romantic now?" They walked out into the balcony. Thomas shook his head, "It is half past midnight. All I see is the dark of the Moon." *Hrijan* was disappointed, "I guess it is better to stay in separate rooms." Thomas was delighted to hear this. He rushed to get his bags and asked the receptionist to take him to one of the spacious rooms on the ground floor. I figured *Hrijan* always had the consolation that his old friend, would appreciate the night sky. But he went to bed with a heavy heart and a single focus, "*Astitva* don't you think Thomas will accompany me to Mr. *Kadar*'s place tomorrow morning?" But I pretended to be asleep.

Kadar's Epilogue

"Chimes of my wrist watch failed to wake me up. All my hopes rested on *Bardaj's* punctuality, and he was asleep on the bench at the reception. However the sound that persuaded me to get up and shut the window belonged to a stranger. Words that he announced on a microphone made no sense. It was fairly dark outside. It appeared the grainy voice wanted to recite a lyric. In a terribly out of sync melody he repeated eight lines of a stanza. Some lines were repeated four times while others only twice. And by the time he finished I heard a knock on my door. As I dragged my feet to open the door *Bardaj's* knock became annoyingly impatient. He was wearing a white coloured skull-cap. "Good morning sir, I got a call from my brother. A taxi will come to pick you up at half past five. Be ready by then and also inform your friends. I would have done it myself but I have to rush to the mosque." *Bardaj* did not even finish the last sentence in the rush. The room was very warm so I decided to take a bath despite the chilly breeze outside. My stock of disposable shaving blades had finished along with my pack of cigarettes so I went upstairs to borrow the blade from *Hrijan* and the cigarettes from *Astitva*. Their door was unlocked. Wet pug marks led to the balcony where *Hrijan* was drying his clothes on ropes provided by the guest house. He was startled to see me, "Well... well..., it isn't even day break and you are already suited up." Weirdly I found myself talking to him in proverbial wisdom, "You know how it is with the early bird and worms." Nonchalantly he replied to it with a smile, "If I did not know better, I would have thought that you didn't sleep at all after our squabble." Of course I had forgotten all about the fight.

Every new day is a new beginning so I told him the truth, "Some lunatic screaming at the top of his tuneless voice ruined my peaceful sleep. Although I am least interested in attending the morning prayers at the monastery I have nothing better to do." *Hrijan* took a cane chair and faced the green dome of the mosque. He offered me to sit next to him so that we could have a word, "It seems that I should thank the men busy in *Adhan* for your company." Incessantly a volley of question sprang at him from my mouth, "So you know who was making that noise. What? Where? Why?" He requested me to face the alley leading to the mosque. At the big juncture sums of men were sitting on the road with their heads bowed. *Hrijan* whispered in my ears, "These men are Mohammedan. The voice you heard belonged to that ecclesiastic sitting in front of them. *Adhan* is a reminder for prayers."

Soon enough our transport arrived. We were going to the neighbouring Buddhist monasteries. *Hrijan* wanted to film the morning prayer of the monks. In the town of *Leh* the roads were empty early morning. The monastery was on the outskirts and it would take a little more than twenty minutes to reach. The prayer was scheduled to begin at half past six and we were awfully early. Surprisingly the driver took us to Mr. *Kadar*, who was returning from the mosque when we reached his office. The room had a work table, a sofa, and an ornamental dining set. Mr. *Kadar* invited us to have breakfast with him. He advised us not to pray on an empty stomach. *Hrijan* sat next to him but refused the mutton, "We are not going to pray. We will observe the monks." Somehow this humoured Mr. *Kadar* who washed his hands before digging in to the platter, "Indeed religion is for a tourist to observe. I reckon the daily visits assist the monks in their quest for nirvana."

After much hesitation I joined *Kadar* for breakfast while *Hrijan* turned his back towards us. Very quietly he discerned the floral depictions on the wall behind the work desk. To bring him out of the trance *Kadar* announced very proudly, "My wife makes them herself, though now she is old and limits to tapestry." *Hrijan* walked closer to the wooden panel, "Indeed she has a very intricate and unwearied hand. If I am not mistaken this is the world renowned Walnut woodcarving of Kashmir valley?" *Kadar* was delighted to meet a patron and replied pompously, "Oh you have an eye for art my friend. This motif in my office always reminds me of our *Nishat Bagh*. The local people call this eloquent art form as *Dhun Hath Kaem*." *Kadar* got up and stood next to the window, "In the peaceful days of the valley our house had a similar window. Our *Abba* bought special frames for each window. The simplistic house had three floors and he spent years in building them one above the other. For those who believe green to be the colour of nature I suggest a week in that white Kashmiri house. Even on the walls of the Sistine Chapel one wouldn't find an equitable assortment of paint. Mother nature would evince the promised heaven every spring. I spent seventeen springs in that house as a Hindu. Then one day when my father came home with a mullah our lives changed forever.

This untidy clergy man had taken upon himself the task to purify us. His very first words to us were not of a pleasant greeting or blessing but of proclamations, "Allah is the Greatest. I testify that there is no God except Allah. I testify that Muhammad is a Messenger of Allah. Prayer is better than sleep. Come to prayer. Come to salvation. Come to success. The time for the best of deeds has come. God is greater than any description. There is no deity except for Allah." He monitored our family daily for months till he was sure that we were purified of our so called sins." *Kadar*'s eyes were seeking the garden out that window. He wanted to peer on either side of that house through that window. And hopefully inhale the scent of blossom from his garden. Tears gleamed in his gray eyes and he continued, "My brothers and I never recited the dawn prayers. As our parents sat there with their eyes closed and head bowed we could not help but wonder at the majesty of the serene Dal lake. *Bardaj* would often ask me if we bowed to the *Pir Panjals*. How could have I told him otherwise? The mullah had placed the Quran in our house and he taught us how to recite it. He mentioned that Allah would be pleased if we mugged it up and recited it five times a day. But he never mentioned the chapter or the page where I could read about the holy city. *Bardaj* would have wanted to know why the city we face was so holy. But the mullah discouraged enquiries and soon I grew accustomed to obey without reason. The same could not be said about my younger brother."

Kadar opened the window with childlike enthusiasm only to find motorcycles parked in front of the 'Refugee Workshop'. Turning around in a tone marred with disappointment he recollected, "On nights when it snowed relentlessly we used the same window as our door. Thus winter introduced itself with a new early morning game. My brother and I would get shovels to toss away the snow that made it impossible to open the gate otherwise. Only we could jump off the window you see." *Hrijan* walked over to *Kadar* and helped him sink into the old willow chair. After closing the window the two of them faced each other for the last time that morning and embraced the truth, "The view has changed a lot my friend."

Monasteries

Even after that epoch from *Kadar* we managed to reach *Thiksey Gompa* in time for the morning prayers. The two of us easily intermingled in a crowd of onlookers appreciating the Buddhist architecture. *Hrijan* was hastily climbing the stairs that led to the main prayer hall. Pretty soon I lost the sight of his rainbow coloured muffler. Of course one couldn't possibly be lost if he knew the way back to the taxi. I could see the taxi as well as the gate to the monastery from where I stood. Suddenly a voice got my attention, "Und diese sind Gebetsmühlen mit Sprechchören auf sieeingraviert. Nach tibetischer Tradition, wenn ein Anhänger nicht rezitieren kann der heiligen Texte, die er ein Rad mit den Mantraseingraviert, um den Segen erhalten können spinnen." The voice had a thick Tibetan accent though it belonged to a blonde man in his early forties. "There are still about twenty minutes before the prayer starts. We will visit the library on the terrace and then the statue of *Maitreya*." I removed my cap and pretended to wander aimlessly and coincidently beside the tourist group. By the size of his stout and supine pace of his dialogue I was convinced he belonged to Austria. However the sun-burnt faces and big cameras around the neck hinted that a majority of his audience was German. The Austrian guide elaborated upon every artefact that we passed. He even explained some of the Buddhist customs and totems like the prayer wheels with chants engraved upon them. According to Tibetan tradition if a devotee cannot recite the holy texts he may spin a wheel with the mantras engraved on it to obtain the blessings. The library was quite small and its doors were shut. He mentioned about ancient texts being preserved there by traditional methodologies without the sophistication of the Vatican library but with equal reverence. Next we headed down to the statue of *Maitreya* but our footsteps were muted by the blaring call of '*Horns of Thiksey*'. "Ladies and *gentleman* please follow me to the prayer hall. We must be seated before the prayer begins. The statue can wait."

The monks were rushing downstairs to the main shrine. Tourists occupied the mats on the floor behind the array of seats on either side of the rectangular hall. Numerous notice boards warned us not to use flash photography inside the dark shady sanctorium. My eyes were searching for *Hrijan* in the room. Soon the room got crowded with swarms of monks. Kindergarten monks running all over the room, arranging the pedestal for elderly monks to sit, composed much of the excitement before the prayer. It would be annoyingly suspicious if I sat next to the German group. My safest bet was a seat right opposite the German travellers on the other side of the room. The view was equally dark from all corners of the hall. The tanned skin of the monks appeared brown at times and their shaved heads had a matte finish.

"Excuse me." An elderly lady sitting by my side had a polite request, "Do you mind taking a picture of my family?" Well I had no problems but I guess the camera would. Many a times the average family vacationers buy inexpensive digital cameras to tag along for exotic trips, however they seldom realize that a detail knowledge of light, motion, sensitivity and exposure is required to take a beautiful picture. The family of five tapered tightly into a warm embrace. The married son invited a child monk to come and sit in his lap. The seven-something boy invited all his friends and they sat all around the family. The family portrait now morphed into an adoption affiche. The camera's viewfinder was all black. I insisted on switching the flash, "Otherwise the photograph would hardly capture the happy expressions on your faces and the gleam sprouting in the toddlers around you." The youngest monk walked over to me. I think he understood English or at least the word 'flash'. With his hand covering the camera he repeated unremittingly, "No flash! No flash!" The owner of the camera explained to the little boy how difficult it would be to take a photograph in the absence of light. His fellow monks also stood up and impassively refused the picture. Only when the elderly woman assured the little boy that we won't use the flash did they allow us to sit in the hall.

Now it was just me and the family with no exploited baby monks and I was about to press the button. He squeaked, "Wait no flash! Wait yes flash." A frustrated German with a tight schedule is not a monk friendly cameraman. Apparently the tot did not know that. He insisted on chiming, "Wait no flash! Wait yes flash." His Mongolic eyes were concerned and stressed. I got up to give the camera back to the Indian family when suddenly the baby monks gathered around me and started counting with their fingers. They wanted me to count with them, "eins, zwei, drei..." the tallest of the boys put his hands on my eyes and continued counting. I recall it was nine when they all just spurted away so that I could complete the count. "Zehn it is!!!"

A blistering sun on the shimmery roof blinded my eyes. An omniscient light source reflected off the golden walls and pillars. The whole room drowned in a sea of light. He wore blue; she was in a tint of orange; my eyes were green and their cheeks were red. Every face in the room gleamed with blessings. Even the monotone monks seemed radiant in the hue of gold. I wish *Hrijan* could see it. He would definitely need to come back tomorrow if he missed this today. My fingers couldn't stop clicking. And I photographed every nook and corner of the hall. Not even the furthest pole was in darkness. An aura was present in the room. No matter how impassable the presence, it was impossible to pinpoint the source of this aura. It could be coming from the gold encased remains of avatars that were housed in this shrine, or the halos of delivered souls that glittered from the beeline of monks in the room. Now I could see everyone in the same light. I could see men who were monks; monks who were boys; boys who were old enough to be men. Some monks were tall while others were stout. Many boys in the room were lost while most men had found. Too many monks who sought were sitting and even more were the number of men, who laughed without seeking. Men who whined and boys who arrived; and they were all visible in the same light. My eyes could see them in the same shade of gold glitter and rainbow for which I needed a flash. I read it in the pamphlet somewhere. The *Thiksey* monastery houses sixty monks at a time. My eyes counted sixty one. The last monk to enter the room had strikingly familiar features which lured me to his side. With pristine diction he recited the holy chants to illuminate the hall with an exuberance unseen in modern times. *Hrijan* traded his multicoloured muffler for a very modest saffron loincloth. I wasn't the only one blinded by admiration and love for *Hrijan*. Every blonde girl in that room requested his company for a tour of the monastery. He obliged none.

For as long as I can remember *Hrijan* has been eager to leave entanglements behind. He transcends into the life of others. Wrapping an unstitched cloth to cover his modesty, taking a pew on the ice cold marble, comprehending mantras from the *Mahavyutpatti* are only a few of the many extremities he was willing to endure so that he can walk where they do, to watch what they see, to listen what they hear and to carve a niche in words that belong to a language he cannot even understand. "It gets warm under the Sun" he explained and unfastened his robe as we stepped into the veranda. The sun illuminated his ruffled mop of hair and shimmered from the teasingly exotic surface of his thirsty lips. "Have you seen the mountains and the Indus valley plains from atop the second roof?" *Hrijan* did not wait for a reply and ran up the staircase. I promised to meet him there once the prayer ceremony was over and he agreed to wait there till it was time to leave.

Reincarnation

As I returned to the main prayer hall the Austrian tourist group was queuing up again. I pretended to tie my shoe laces till the last member of the group climbed the narrow staircase. Hastily I ran across the porch. Thanks to the snarly pace of the toddlers travelling with them I was able to reach the statue of *Maitreya* just in time. The West facing door was made of pure gold. The gold plated statue was housed in a three storey temple. A bedazzled Paula asked the guide if this is was the statue of Lord Gautama Buddha. The guide asked little Paula to come closer and listen intently. "Common to the canonical literature of all Budhist sects is a prophecy. Forestalled to a time and age when the *Dharma* will seem to be forgotten from the face of this earth. *Maitreya* will appear on Earth, achieve complete enlightenment, and teach the pure *dharma*. Much has been written about his guiding hand, his radiant crosses and circles of enlightenment. Everyone in this world is hoping that someone from somewhere will come to renounce all their fears. Unknowingly we all have already worshipped him in some form or the other without heaving his teachings."

His statuette was embellished with ornaments. A calming smile distracted us from his closed eyes. In deep meditation, the figurine took little notice of a German visitor and an inquisitive Austrian toddler. His legs were crossed in an *asana* which wasn't visible till we peeped down to the ground floor. The artist had tucked his tresses behind the ear so that *Maitreya* may hear prayers of the bowing pilgrims. This completed our guided tour of *Thiksey* monastery. The German speaking Tibetan guide closed the door as he counted the last of the Austrian tourists.

I was alone with *Maitreya* for a few minutes and he was in no hurry to arrive. Only a cataclysmic turn of events could persuade him to redeem his followers. This building was full of people who had fled their homeland or forsaken their families. Some followers abandoned an economist's society to be a part of a very different order up here in the mountains where money should ideally mean paper. I was yet to meet a believer among these followers. *Hrijan* was back to take me away from this carpeted room. He had changed back into his black woollens and the multicoloured muffler. He opened the door. The Sun shone brightly behind his back and I bowed to his formless beauty, I guess it was acceptable to see God in love. "

Thomas was yet to share his personal opinion. While doing so he looked at the cloudy sky and moved away from *Hrijan*. He rebuked from his raptness with a laugh, "I am sure the monks at the monastery got their story right. Someone several centuries ago must have brought a Bible to their king. Needless to say the monks unwittingly look forward to the imminent return of the son, Jesus Christ. Who will once again preach to some, forgive many and serve all." Age could not suppress *Atiik's* aggression and with a crisscrossed forehead he argued, "You secularist pigs will never forgo infidelity. Come judgement day the Twelfth *Imam Muhammad Al-Mahdi* will return from occultation. In numbers never seen before Mohammedans will rise together. He will guide our souls against all evil idol worshippers. Those who do not believe Allah to be the one true God will be wiped off from the face off this Earth." It pained *Tenzing* to hear such violent prophecies of Islam. Expecting that night to be his last stand against any sort of oppression he explained to *Atiik's* nephews, "*Maitreya* advocates peace. Armed with compassion and faith. Please don't address Non-Mohammedans odiously. Any enlightened being would abstain from hatred." *Atiik* had lost his breath in the heated argument and he needed his youngest nephew to lift him up from the seat. *Salman* had blind faith in every word the old man said, "Nonviolence, benevolence and enlightenment are the mechanics of a coward. The holy Quran is a book of peace. It states all men are brothers. If our brothers withdraw from the righteous path of the all powerful Allah it becomes our duty to steer them back." *Hasaan* added to *Salman's* interpretation of the holy book, "Quran empowered the Mughals to kill any infidel so that he may turn to Islam for the fear of his life. The book entitles a Mohammedan to virgins, for Allah knows the source of all pleasure. Jihad knows no boundary. Great Muhammad waged a war for ten long years to turn all of Arabia into the Mohammedan haven that it is today. He united the land by the sword and so shall be the way ahead." This morning when we decided to occupy the roof of this motel a silent mutual covenant was signed. In order to survive the flood stricken province we must work together. Some volunteered to clean while others cooked. Many lifted the deceased from under the debris. We had witnessed enough of life and death in the last twelve hours to extract cooperation. However the very premise of religion was either to unite a majority or the upheaval of a subjugated minority. The flooding water was not the only demon on the roof.

Sahishnu and *Shamasheel* had worries that were shared only by me. *Shamasheel* being the fatherly figure tried to calm us. In an address directed towards all the angry men on the roof he told his brother, "All of them have a plan. Mohammedans will multiply incessantly until the judgement day comes. Jews seek revenge for Man slaughter. Christians have monetized the world in a bid to privatize world peace. Yet each one of them longs for either a patronizing multinational media-corporate nexus or the approval of a jihadist war lord. They are scared to take up the responsibility of their actions. Hence they go by the words written in a book. Ironically it is supposed to be the same book. Every religion claims that the author instigated their faith in an ever so perfect entity called God. These books house a huge stack of excuses to choose from. Every follower finds impunity in his favourite book." On the roof, that night when death came upon us, we were all looking up at the heavens for appraisal. Some were content with a very long uneventful existence while others were frustrated with mediocrity. Complacency had seeped into the peace-seekers as they grew accustomed to an increasingly hostile society. I am a Hindu visiting the border town of *Leh*. And I am scared because my God will wait for a million years to come to this Earth and leave an everlasting first impression. Such tempestuous premises brought upon us by the demoniac religions of Central Asia require summoning of the pristine Hindu who resides in every non-belligerent heart.

Antiphony

The air was poisoned by our venomous verbal skill. For another hour or two there were no words exchanged. Only an antiphon of snobbish noses, provocative gestures, racial insults, and affronting glances. The fire had lost its warmth. It even stopped giving light. In fact nobody cared to light it up. Once again the gods blared at us from up above the clouds. *Hrijan* stepped forward with a large log of wood. It was way too heavy for him to lift, so he dragged it along the floor. In his passage *Hrijan* made a point to hit every hurdle he could recognize with his foot. Quite similar to the ictus after a downbeat he caught everyone's attention. *Shamasheel* was the first one to stand up and assist *Hrijan*. Together they lifted the log above the ground which allowed the silence to resurface. And just before we all fell into the chill of hostility again he began to sing, "One woodpecker chewing it down, along came another and two chewed on... Two woodpeckers..." They placed the log on a granite platform. *Hrijan* held the log from one side while *Shamasheel* went looking for the axe in the debris. *Tenzing* brought a smile to their frowning faces when he realized that he was sitting on the carpenter's box. He drew out a saw from the magical box. Now the three of them raised the tempo of *Hrijan's* song, "Two woodpeckers looking for a bark, in the night all alone when it was dark, along came another with the sharpest beak of all... Three woodpeckers... chewing on the bark" It was a pathetic effort I tell you on *Tenzing's* part. He sat on the log and tried to saw it down from the centre. *Hrijan* and *Shamasheel* strenuously gripped either ends of the log. But it was just not fast enough and the bonfire was dying out. He shredded a few pieces here and there which were collected by Thomas. He was going to try and rekindle the fire when *Atiik* stopped his hand. Though he was not polite to the foreigner but his words smelt of wisdom, "The wood is damp. Dry it in the flames first." Thomas handed over the twigs to *Atiik*. He asked his children and nephews to collect newspaper, dry cotton or anything that can burn. He put all of it in the fire. First the very short chips were added, and then he dried the bigger ones by holding them over the flame. On the other side of the fire our three woodpeckers were not struggling anymore. *Salman* was swinging in complete harmony with *Tenzing* as they sawed off the wood into half, then a fourth and so on. Upon concentrating I could even hear his line of the song. Once the fire turned yellow again *Daya* brought some oil to assist the flame. Now that we had plenty of wood to last the night I found the axe. It was under the granite platform on which *Hrijan* had placed the log. Having noticed it before him I got the chance to swing one last time and chop off the last piece of wood. Most of us were tired now so *Hrijan* did not need to strain his voice to be audible, "When we stop sharing, this fire loses its warmth. No light can come off it, if we shut the windows of our heart. Your unlettered rubberneck sends a chill down my spine. My existence is mulled over by your actions of antagonism. This flame reduces to ash if this hostile dialogue is prolonged. So stop thinking, avoid confronting and continue with your work. Leave religion for those who need to follow and find spirituality inside of you and in your actions." *Hrijan* bowed away from the roof as if he was expecting someone. Maybe he was giving us some time to contemplate and then suddenly turned around to announce, "Find *Bardaj*, he might want to hear this." A motorcycle stopped below the guest house. Most of us found it hard to recognize the rider. He collapsed right at the doormat.

"Sprinkle some water." "I say let him drink water." "The city just witnessed a flood. Water is the last thing he wants to taste." "Will soda do?"

He woke up startled in our bed on 8th August 2010. *Tenzing* was worried and questioned *Jenso*, "Where are the others? Why have you come alone?" Thomas suspected that *Jenso* had returned to take *Tenzing* back along with him. However the wet clothes and broken helmets narrated a different story. He hastily gulped a bottle of orange soda. It took an entire day for the bed sheets to dry and this man had soiled them again. *Atiik* asked *Daya* to open the windows. Mountains were vaguely visible in the distant horizon and the thunder rattled the window frame. *Jenso* reacted rather violently to this sight and sound. Gripping me by the collar he shouted frantically for us to shut the windows, "*Shamar*! It's too heavy. We must return. *Shamar* you won't make it. It's rain. It's all around. Shut the door, shut the window it will flood your house. Run with us. Leave it, it's a storm." *Tenzing* stood up and shut the doors and windows, "All right it's over now. I have closed the windows." Upon hearing *Tenzing's* voice distinctly for the first time after waking up *Jenso* calmed down. He crawled up to the side of the bed and whispered, "*Tenzing* my brother, don't go outside. The water takes no prisoners." And he collapsed again. *Tenzing* couldn't get over the shock. He fell on the floor holding *Jenso's* hand. After the recent squabble on the roof no one cared to console him. The silence was broken only when *Hrijan* entered the room with a fresh pair of clothes. He had the commiseration of a nurse in his manner, "Everybody outside please. Only one man should stay here with me. We will get him into dry clothes. You can all interrogate him later." The brothers from *Mysore* were very eager to leave. *Tenzing* was still gaping at his unconscious comrade. I rushed out of the room as soon as he removed *Jenso's* trousers.

After half an hour of arguments inside that room *Hrijan* resurfaced with a shaman like graveness, "This man is in shock. We will have to wait till he is wide awake." *Tenzing* was dragging his heavy heart across the floor when *Hrijan* asked him for a favour, "*Jenso* has a lot to tell us. It would be great if you could also find *Bardaj* by the time he is conscious." Ignoring *Hrijan's* request *Tenzing* marched on to the roof. Having nothing good to do we were going to join him upstairs. Following our footsteps *Atiik* emerged from the room along with *Sahishnu* and Thomas. In a concerned voice he told his sons, "Come with us to look for *Bardaj*." All of us were shocked and *Khurram* raised a voice, "So you will be taking orders from an infidel now." Thomas found it to be a cretinous response; however he did not voice any such concerns and ignored them with a smirk. *Sahishnu* never expected any sort of co-operation from Mohammedans so he walked out with

Thomas. *Atiik* was saddened by this remark and asked his eldest son to walk him out, "It is not a surprise that *Khurram* considers helping a Hindu as servitude. We tutored him to label every non-Mohammedan as an infidel. But the man who requests us to fetch *Bardaj* is not an infidel. He looks for God in self-effacing acts of empathy. He is never loud, lest his voice might be considered noise." I was shocked to see that *Atiik* had developed a distinctive affection for *Hrijan*. "Oh but it is way beyond fondness. I revere his sublime presence." *Hasaan* was convinced that his old man had lost his mind yet he tried to persuade him back to rationale, "*Abba*, he is a twenty year old Hindu boy who has travelled all the way from New Delhi to Ladakh just to meet his friend. He has not performed any miracles and I do not see a halo above his head. Remember how every prophet had heavenly powers. Quran is full of such stories." *Salman* obeyed *Atiik's* order and went out to look for *Bardaj*. As for his younger brothers a lot of learning was yet to be accomplished, "Did it ever occur to you that none of us know the name of his friend? He never tells us about the message he has been sent to convey. Nor do we know who the addresser is. For all we know it could be an excuse for the almighty to bring us together. The books we revere tell us of men who accomplished the antemundane and established a religion in the process, for us to follow. You seek a miracle to believe in his divinity. Many of them have already gone unnoticed under your unsuspecting faith. Try listening and believing the next time he talks. A man guiding you in person is worth far more than a book authored by old men centuries ago."

I returned to the room where *Shamasheel* and *Hrijan* were looking after *Tenzing's* companion. They were lying on the carpet. *Shamasheel* was weeping.

Shamasheel, "You know I have a wife?"

Hrijan, "Of course, you already mentioned that."

Shamasheel, "But she is a middling. Not as beautiful as any of the women you get to sleep with."

Hrijan, "You don't mean that. Moreover do I look a like a man whose idea of heaven is centred around seventy two virgins." And both of them cracked on the floor laughing at their miserable sense of humour.

Shamasheel was still not finished whining.

Shamasheel, "I have a brother."

Hrijan, "I kind of noticed that."

Shamasheel, "Did you also notice that he is a lost cause without me?"

Hrijan agreed with him, "Of course, that is why you must not leave him."

Shamasheel, "Even I don't plan to do so but some day I plan to live my life."

Hrijan, "Does that life feature a motorcycle ride across the colourful abode of nature? Perhaps a makeshift raft skillfully manoeuvred down a torrent and a dive in the limitless oceans of the world to look for that one perfectly formed pearl."

Shamasheel, "Yes all that and a lot more. Not long ago I was also very brave. I would have cancelled my return flights. Even I would jump off a raft to fetch the necklace of a fair maiden. Would you believe me if I told you that my favourite part in this adventure was the confrontation of a Neo-Nazi and a Tibetan? I could be all that you are."

Hrijan, "How do you know all this?"

Shamasheel, "I bought the tickets you cancelled. The flight should have left this morning but somehow the airport was not serviceable."

Hrijan, "The *Spirit* thought that I would deter from my path and take the flight. He has lost his faith in me I guess."

Shamasheel wanted to know more about *Hrijan's* mystical friend. He suggested they go and meet him together. Seemingly this middle aged man was reaching out to people around him. His eyes beamed at the bleak possibility of meeting *Hrijan's* friend. *Shamasheel* explained,

"I am not eager to go home. I will cancel my ticket and then both of us can stay here. I promise..."

Hrijan did not let *Shamasheel* finish. He got up and checked on *Jenso*. This conversation was over when they saw me. But *Shamasheel* had one last question, "Why don't you post the letter?"

Hrijan was obliged to reply, "I am still alive. Consider me to be a postman in the age of email. Once I deliver this letter I will fulfill my purpose and that would be the end of me."

Shadows in the room engraved *Shamasheel's* corner as he enquired about his own fate. Essaying the perfect brother had been his purpose after the demise of their father. One day *Sahishnu* would free his elder brother of this obligation. Sooner than he would suspect his daughter would also be married off to a suitable boy. Will God take all this away from him? *Shamasheel's* voice had suddenly lost its enthuse. Without a cauldron of responsibility a man loses his will to live. Most men fill this cauldron by the virtue of their actions. So the more eccentric your actions are the less trite your existence is. This is not a dictionary definition of freedom. Man always looks for excuses to abstain from the bond of love, emotions, and responsibilities in order to attain a neo-liberal lifestyle. However freedom is a hitherto unparalleled event only when your existence is devoid of purpose.

"*Tenzing*, I am cold. Oh... why is it so cold?" *Jenso* was shivering and *Hrijan* could not comfort him with blankets. *Shamasheel* suggested that we carry him upstairs. He weighed considerably less in a fresh pair of dry clothes. *Tenzing* did not acknowledge our presence on the roof. Not until *Jenso* lay next to him hemmed with several layers of blankets. All of us stared into the fire. For an hour no words were exchanged. The silence was broken by sporadic footsteps of our eldest companion. *Atiik* returned with his sons and nephews. They failed to find *Bardaj*. *Jenso* was conscious now. He wanted to talk, however *Tenzing* wasn't listening. So I moved closer to this young man who was about to enter the afterlife very soon. "I can see", were the first words from *Jenso's* mouth that reassured us of the stability of his condition. *Atiik* stepped forward, "Yes, what can you see?" *Jenso* turned to face the elderly Mohammedan. For the first time I saw a man who closed his eyes to narrate what he saw, "I can see the sky is blue and white. If I go along this road any further I will be in no man's land. The villagers told us that soldiers from either side can shoot us down there." His voice resembled a newly born girl child as he spoke of death, "I can see we are not scared. The water near my feet is green and cold. It has no medicinal significance and nobody recommended us to bathe here." He was shivering in his dream, "I can see that *Hrijan* has the longest throw. His stone skips past the green boundary and disappears into the ever expanding blue water." A whisper in my ear reminded me of similar sights. He was revisiting memories of the past few days. *Jenso* gazed at the dark skies this time, "While I still stood knee deep in that lake wondering how cold the blue water must be *Hrijan* swam across to the other side. He disappeared from our sights." This young Tibetan warrior brought a smile on our faces for the last time that night. Of course I had come to terms with *Hrijan's* slipperiness. No matter how hard I gripped onto him, he always grew a bigger set of wings. By this time Thomas returned with *Sahishnu*. Unable to find *Bardaj* they sat on the same side as *Atiik*. Thomas listened intently as *Jenso* mentioned his name.

"I can see another one of those Bavarian tourists who are fond of the silvery water. Unfortunately we have to cross the Indian borders to taste that mysterious juice. Thomas walked gullibly hand in hand with *Hrijan* as far as my eyes could see and beyond. But they returned in a hurry." Thomas did not endorse this stereotype of a German tourist in *Leh*. Even he realized that *Jenso* was recalling our placid trip to *Spangmik* village on the shores of *Pangong* Lake. The salty lake, that is divided obtusely by the Line of actual control between India and China, provided an opportunity for the nomadic tribesmen to share their tents with well paying tourists. Unlike us, those rich tourists needn't return the same afternoon. They could savour the mottled waters of this inland basin in deluxe tents all day. This single dimensional description of the heavenly hues caught *Tenzing's* attention.

What else did he see? Everyone wanted to know. And so *Jenso* raised his voice, "I can see angry rain gods. We were over confident of our driving skills. Maybe we wanted an opportunity to prove that this trip was possible even without your leadership. We were so wrong.

Danny asked us to remove our helmets. With such heavy rains it was impossible to see the road or the valley or even ourselves from the limited scope of the visor. That was our first mistake. The military forces had spent the whole night trying to repair the bridge but all in vain. They never anticipated such heavy rains. We expected to ride clear off the roads on our motorcycles. Just imagine how much space would a bike need? But the road that leads to Srinagar is battered so badly that even military supplies have been cut off." I looked at *Hrijan*. Up till now *Bardaj's* absence had not hindered the relevance of *Jenso's* chronicle. *Tenzing* wanted *Jenso* to rest but he went on with his confession, "*Kadar* claimed to know several goat passes. He insisted we follow him. Up on that route we were the solo travellers. *Shamar* was the first one to lose balance. He fell on his beautiful face. Even before we could get off our motorcycles to see his bruised nose his motorcycle followed him. *Kadar* did not leave his vehicle. There was no time to scream for help and no one who would listen. *Shamar's* bag was heavy enough to drag him along with the motorcycle into the valley below." With big needy eyes *Jenso* looked at the four men from Mysore who stared right back at him without any sympathy. In a trembling voice he continued, "The second strike of thunder swallowed *Kadar's* car. His hatchback had little chance against the behemoth wave of the rushing mud-spattered water. We vowed to look after each other. However, after looking at the peculiar inclination at which *Kadar's* car was stuck on the slope below, I maintained a considerable distance. This did not stop *Danny*. He searched my backpack to find a rope. One end of the rope was fastened to a tree while *Danny* hung to the other end of the rope. With very small steps he rappelled down. *Kadar* was still conscious, though he was not screaming for help. One wholesome look at the stream that had formed in the valley below could mute even the bravest of hearts. I presume he lost all hope when his bottom hit the windshield of the car. Unexpectedly even in such circumstances *Kadar* argued with *Danny*. He wanted to carry his briefcase. It could have contained clothes, money or food. Whatever it might have been, it was not worth the time under those circumstances. I begged them to return. Neither of them took my advice seriously. My motorcycle had no luggage or pillion. And so I turned around. At the third strike of thunder I deserted both of them. The engine of my motorcycle charred in unison with the lightning bolt that banished the tree forever." *Tenzing* offered his lap to the tiring head of *Jenso*. They hugged each other and opened their hearts to grief and soon *Jenso* succumbed to his injuries. *Tenzing's* cloak was wet with tears.

The members on the rooftop filled the air surrounding them with emotions. Their caldron of guilt, denial, resentment, accusation and confession was empty. Some proved they were heroes; others were ashamed of their heroics. A resounding silence exclaimed that we had nothing to say. The words from our lips had left them parched. Every phrase had been heard as if it was our last.

Hrijan got up from his seat and opened up his backpack. He completed a circle around the bonfire and offered from his backpack a piece of chocolate pie to each one of us. No one cared to thank him. That night we shared a lot more than just stories. We considered ourselves worthy of all the abundance that the world offered and a 'chocpie' topped that list. I got the second last piece. It was still hard to bite off. So I nibbled on the crumbs. *Hrijan* returned to his spot next to the fire. He unwrapped the white foil and devoured each little marshmallow patiently. None of us were in a hurry, we had no meetings to attend; no appointments to honour; no commitments to fulfil yet the 'chocpie' disappeared down our bellies before *Hrijan* chewed his first bite.

Sahishnu had sulked next to his brother. Probably he wished to be sitting next to his wife. She would have been thrilled at the prospects of spending their last night cushioning each other in the chilly mountains as they stared into a bonfire. He missed her worrisome nagging.

Tenzing could use some beer now. After losing all the members of his biker gang he crouched like a conquered general. The political party he represented yielded a cosh and prayed for a righteous death. This however was too soon. He was yet to be imprisoned or wounded in battle. No freedom struggle could end at the hands of Mother Nature. His eyes were longing for some godly hope as they traced the old mountain trail leading down to the bus stand.

Thomas had no intentions of complaining. For the first time in this entire trip he was sitting on the floor. Very hesitantly he removed his contact lenses. Now there was no hope of a rescue mission that would be telecast on international news so he preferred his spectacles. A flashlight fumbled out of his bag as he secured his lenses.

Shamasheel did not give into fear anymore. He patted his younger brother as if assuring his son of returning home, no matter what. Probably the only man left on that roof who was not lurking into the past anymore. He had definite hope that his wits would lead them safely home. For once he did not miss his wife or children. I could see the assertion on his face.

Daya was unperturbedly finishing off the chores. The owner's brother had worked for fifteen years in *Leh*, sometimes even till late winter months of October-November. No rainstorm would change that. *Daya* never complained, rather he served us all day. When we all die I am pretty sure he would be the one with the least disgruntlement. He had announced earlier that there would be no dinner but nevertheless he was back with some herbal tea.

Atiik murmured a prayer audible only to the Mohammedans sitting around him. They were good Mohammedans who helped us in the morning. They brought the very little food which we ate. Seemingly awkward was the inability to understand their prayers. A holy communion after our last supper should have involved people from all faiths.

Many books tell stories of nights such as this. This night is long enough to recall all of them. *Hrijan* stood up from his place and went downstairs. Probably he had to use the bathroom, but he came back rather quickly and this time he wasn't alone. The youngest girl from the dislocated family was sobbing in his arms. He asked her to sit exactly at the spot which he preferred. She was happy to be next to the fire and *Hrijan* asked her, "Why do you cry little angel?" The girl had no reservations in conversing with this stranger, "My friends went up that side towards the haunted fort. I am yet to hear from them." *Hrijan* stepped onto the last stone towards the far edge of the roof and produced a mouth organ from his pocket, "Your friends are there, I see them. Would it comfort you if they heard us?" Without waiting for a nod from the little girl he played the organ.

Till date I have never heard symphonies from Mozart or ragas from *Tansen*. Yet I will go on and compare them to this young man in his early twenties. He blew profusely into the organ and waited for the echo to come back. The girl smiled at every octave the mountains all around the valley mirrored. He turned swiftly and whispered, "So young lady do you see our friends are all around and all of them have a mouth organ to play."

"Did you see that?" *Shamasheel* asked a sleeping *Sahishnu*, "Did anyone see that?" Thomas was the first one to confirm the sighting. I pleaded that we did not need to stage a play to hoodwink a little girl but *Atiik* had also joined the commotion. *Tenzing* quickly borrowed the flashlight from Thomas and repeatedly blinked it towards the mountain. He continued to do so till the batteries were completely drained.

Daya complained, "I tell you these Chinese flashlights courtesy our friend Sherpa are a blot on the very word technology. They shouldn't even be sold in the first place."

"Great going *Tenzing*; that was our last source of light in case the fire burns out." And suddenly as if the Gods were responding to every word Thomas said that night, it began to rain. It rained till the last lath turned black as coke and then it rained a little more and when everyone went indoors to the third floor it stopped. It was dark and my only priority was to find *Hrijan*. All through my life I cared for no one, in fact I really did not care for *Hrijan* either; yet I couldn't possibly return without him. And we heard exasperations from the entire room. The dislocated family woke up and all three of their children began to cry. *Tenzing* and Thomas were still fiddling with the flashlight and the old man was being carried by his prodigies. *Hrijan* was still waiting for us on the roof. He was trying to restart the fire but in vain. The clouds gave no room to the moon and the night was darker then his eyes. Nobody helped him to start a fire but he gathered more wood and he lit it one at a time. The rain washed off all the emotions that stuffed the roof a minute ago. It was a blank slate now. A blank black slate waiting for *Hrijan* and he began by lighting the fire.

"There it is I see it. Oh my god they are returning." *Salman* could not control the thrill in his voice. We all looked in the direction *Tenzing* was pointing and saw several cars returning back from the hills. *Atiik* stared at the haunted fort which was bubbling with flashlights blinking and signalling that we have survived. "Look it is the car of the owner."

Thomas hailed into the by lane. Only one headlight was functional. The paint made way for a rusty metallic body. As the driver bubbled the car to a halt the owner's younger brother emerged from the hind seat. With his hunkered shoulders and heavy feet he carried a dark brown briefcase. Probably if it would have not been that dark we would have never spotted those ushering flashlights or the headlamps of cars returning home.

Bardaj ordered the dislocated family to move out. He joined the remaining occupants on the roof. Grief dulled his face as he sat next to the coffee tray. *Daya* offered him a fresh cup which he politely refused. *Atiik* sat next to him, "I believe your brother did not make it." *Bardaj* jumped out of his seat, "No he did not and all of you will. I asked him to sit and wait in the mosque but he had plans, business plans. Now he won't see me ever again. He has been swallowed by the galloping stream of water. My brother is no more. Oh Allah! My brother is no more. Go away! The water has subsided and soon roads will be functional. All of you can sleep and tomorrow a new day will begin and you all can go home."

His was not the only wailing voice that night. Children were orphaned, young girls widowed, men amputated and sons were smothered in the first flood that the city of *Leh* witnessed. But all of us went to bed that night; all of us but one, the one who seeks an audience with a man staying on the other side of the valley. A dark night was lit on that secluded roof with the refulgence of nine lives. All nine lives but one, *Hrijan* did not have anything to narrate all day. Yet I never noticed signs of intimidation on his serene façade. He chose to sit next to the fire; Next to the source of all brilliance and choose to keep quiet. His eyes reflected the splendour of nine miserable existences.

Return

"Allah O' Akbar..." I woke up next to a coffee mug which smelt of green tea. The window was open and the drapes wet. I peeped outside. No rain, no cloud, no sun. It could start raining any moment. That would definitely wash the tears of town-folk. The room was empty and someone was in the bathroom. Our suitcases were neatly packed and stacked one above the other on the bed besides his pillow. Maybe he did not sleep last night. I recall he was sitting on the writing desk when he asked me to sleep. In his neatly spaced running hand I could see scribbling on an off white sheet of handmade paper, "*For our people I may say my work cannot end, hence in a sense I cannot retire as long as peace needs a prose and patience needs practice. For only then can a 'human' be 'kind'.*" Ah Darn this boy, I could have never guessed what kept him up the whole night?

As I proceeded to knock on the bathroom there was another knock. It was from the outside and on the front door. I requested Thomas to march in. After the floods we had stopped bolting doors. He was in his trekking gear that consisted of his signature cap covering a bald patch and detachable cargos. He had two backpacks now, the little one had been specifically bought two days ago for touring the city. He stood there for a moment staring at my pyjamas before asking, "*Astitva* you don't plan to go to the airport like that, do you?"

Hrijan sprung out of the bathroom and hit my head with the door. *Hrijan* was as dappered as Thomas, maybe more. "All set mate, everything has been worked out. Unfortunately no taxi is operational so we walk to the airport" he gestured with high steps as he picked up the lighter suitcase, "*Bardaj* is mourning his dead brother so I paid the pending amount to *Daya*. Still I have eleven thousand rupees left with me." I wasn't given a decent amount of time to get ready, only enough to wear my clothes. My bag was heavy and still wet. It made the long walk to the airport aching.

Thomas never started conversations but today our chatterbox needed stimulus, "I am sorry *Hrijan*. I sincerely wanted you to meet the man on the other side of the valley."

"It is just fine." *Hrijan* was always prompt with his replies.

Thomas continued, "Will you come back for him? Did you inform him that we leave today? I am sure he will understand."

"Yes he will understand" *Hrijan* would always stare in the eyes while talking, "though I had a lot more for him to hear and contemplate." Nobody knew who this man waiting for him on the other side was. He phrased words with every step one at a time, "Last night I saw your demons. Each and every one of you faced it. None of us were alone, we faced all the demons together. Only when we face them together do we ever conquer them." Thomas very emphatically agreed with *Hrijan*, "I am glad I had you by my side when my demons surfaced."

Hrijan wasn't talking to us anymore, "He needs to know this too. He must already know this but he is waiting. Spirits told me that he was waiting. My obligation was to face him and show him a mirror. I tell you we are much the same. However he is the only one yielding the sabre, The Sabre of Peace. Well I guess Spirits will have to look for another day and another messenger."

I could no longer suppress my curiosity, "Who was the man on the other side of the valley?"

"Hey stop! Come on both of you." Thomas had stopped paying attention to *Hrijan's* philosophy long ago. In fact he yelled for a taxi whilst I asked the most intriguing question. He bargained directly with the driver, "All I can pay you are these godforsaken Euros. We need to get to the airport and fast." I looked at his hands that tempted the driver, who resembled our very own *Sherpa*. "We don't need your money. Just get in. We are also headed to the airport" answered an elderly couple sitting alone in the 8-seater taxi. We piled up our baggage on the roof. Thomas and I were sitting beside the driver while *Hrijan* faced the couple. Their fourth honeymoon was rather short lived. The man sounded very euphoric about a flood spoiling their party. "They make such stuff only in the movies", he said. But his wife was whining. She planned to return home with a baby girl this time. As I turned around to see her whimpered cheeks I realised she was quite young and the man was most probably her father or rather her father's age. They were French and came all the way to India for a romantic holiday. A terrible time to come I say. They got a bumpy ride in this zooming taxi. In fact the driver was talking at the same pace as the car. He was being paid extra by the couple to come early that morning yet he couldn't show up with a smile. This was his early morning tour of the city, "Aah... the local school sir. This road leads to the caved-in bus top. Over there is our grandest hotel. I come to this restaurant often to have lunch. Dinner is savoured best at home." Talking of home I recall perfectly what he meant. Seven days in this awfully arid climate had taken its toll on our skin, wits and our appetite. We had been eating chocpies for over a night now. "And madam the road on the left leads to *Choglamsar*, the official residence of His Holiness The 14th Dalai Lama. We will take the road next to it leading straight to the airport. On any other occasion I start my day by bowing at the monasteries. Well that won't happen today. You need to get to the airport and I need to get paid. There has been no business for last two days you know."

"Stop Stop... Will you just stop the car... Please! I get off here." *Hrijan* interrupted the driver's monologue. "What? You want me to stop here at the Sonam Norboo Memorial hospital. You are awfully early for regular visiting hours. Man! I cannot stop." *Hrijan* got off the car. He took out a sheet of paper from his bag and handed the bag to me. He smiled at the elderly couple and the driver, "Thank you very much" He looked me in the eyes and told me to take his suitcase to the airport, "I will be joining you shortly." I had to stop him, "Where do you think you are going young man. I cannot return without you. What if you don't make it in time for the flight? How will I face your family when I return to Delhi? So you just step back into the car please." The driver gave no time for his mind to change and pressed on the throttle. He did answer and I cannot recall but it had something to do with our money.

Airport

At the airport already hundreds of tourist had gathered. If one wanted he could divide the travellers into three groups. The ones who were inside the airport waiting to check in. They had tickets, boarding passes and were waiting for the first flight to land. The second line was outside the ticket counter. This is where we queued up. People were waiting for the counter to open. The third category was the most docile. They had booked tickets and their flight was to come late in the afternoon. So they would just have to stroll the premises of the airport till then. Hours went by and our queue got shorter. The counter was yet to open. Thomas' patience was wearing out. No clear announcement was made regarding the availability of seats in the departing flights. Frustration was mounting on our faces. Thomas had finished all the water bottles that we were carrying. I could do anything for a drop of water right now and I think the heavens were eavesdropping. It began to rain again. This time most people were ready with umbrellas and raincoats. I was not one of them. Soon my sweater was wet. I could not stand in the chill any longer. And just when my patience was running out the ticket counter adjacent to our queue opened. There was only one flight available for immediate departure. Fishyqueen Airlines was selling tickets to men, women and children who were stranded in the flood struck region. People were pleased by the devotion of this private airline. They were charging twenty two thousand rupees for each ticket. I checked *Hrijan's* bag. He always kept his money in the centre pocket. I counted all the loose currency notes. They amounted to a little more than eleven thousand. ATMs had not been functional the previous afternoon and the ticket counter only accepted crisp green notes, no credit whatsoever.

People shoved us out of the queue. Though the authorities had claimed to have enough seats to get everyone out of the city, the throng of tourists that had convened at the airport was impatient, abusive and uncooperative. Understandably everyone wanted to buy the first ticket. Thomas lost all hope, "I always wanted to be rescued by a helicopter but it seems even the rescue missions in India are commercialized." He lifted his rucksack and returned to the hotel. He did not say good bye and I decided not to accompany him. Furthermore *Hrijan* would meet me here, he promised. Even as I stood there stranded on the airport our military trucks were rebuilding the highways, clearing the runway and offering medical assistance to the injured. My hopes were riding high on their adroitness. Maybe in another two days the small town of *Leh* would be reconnected to the rest of the country.

Run, run for your lives! It's the water! People rushed into the airport lobby. By passers and taxi drivers scaled the walls and entered the safe premise of the landing field. People were praying in languages I did not understand; to a God I had full faith in. Every face had exactly the same expression. The little girl whose fancy lace coat got entangled in my belt was weeping. She had lost her doll in the tumult. While most men panicked leading to the possibility of a stampede, the men in uniform displayed camaraderie. The Indo-Tibetan Border Police, the Border Security force and the Indian Army were busy building up defences to withstand an environment taking up offence against the inhabitants. Some men were carrying sand bags to the gates. Others who had a shovel filled sand into those bags. Rest collected bags to put sand in them. It took mere twenty minutes for them to secure the airport against an impending flood. And while all of us waited inside the concrete building of the airport our army monitored the entry and exit gates. I realised that my suitcases were still outside. More men came rushing from the main road and claimed to be chased by a colossal wave. But water was not visible in the vicinity. It had to be a rumour or some insane man's imagination spawning from fear. The same fear had manifested in our hearts and it appeared we could hear the water as it hurried towards us. A minute had passed with our guards down. The gates of the airport opened for a military truck. The truck was empty and was destined to carry out relief work in distant provinces which had been affected by the floods. Four men alighted from the truck. All of them wore different uniforms and another gentleman in mufti got down from the trunk of the truck. They marched to the side door and entered the ticket counter. People gladdened as the announcement for the departure of the first flight was made. We were waiting for it to return and then rescue the second wave of estranged tourists. The entry gates reopened and the man in mufti walked in first. He had a doll in his hand and he jumped atop a trolley to address the befuddled travellers.

"Let us lose the doubts." He brandished the doll above his head and the little girl rushed towards him. She nearly toppled him from the trolley. But he maintained his balance and continued talking, *"The torrents of our cravings will be cut off. We ought to be free from all misery and only then can we manage to cross the ocean of becoming."* People had started leaving the lobby but he was not finished, *"Lead a holy life. No longer regard anything as your own. How good were your possessions, your gold or silver, your home, your relatives?"* By the time he reached his last but second stanza a queue had formed outside the ticket counter again. His voice shot from trebles of distraught to low notes of appeal, *"Tear the net of passion, lead a life in trance, and there will be an abundance of joy and happiness, for we will lead a holy life."*

People never let *Hrijan* finish his discourse and disperse almost as soon as he says the final word. I waited for him to find me. He always finds me. Our tickets were visibly yoked to the pen pocket of his brown coloured sling bag. He signalled me to get the remaining suitcases which were lying outside in the drizzle.

I asked him, "What took you so long?"

He smiled back, "The only operational ATM in this city was somewhere in the cantonment area."

Me, "So you walked all the way to get the money for our tickets?"

"No, the army truck spotted me as I finally posted the letter."

Afterword

This is an abridged version of the book. Each character had several more pages to occupy. Probably you have met similar personas in your daily life. It is about time you befriend them. Remember the only way to fight our demons is to face them together. Don't be a stranger anymore. Hopefully, unlike the ten men on the roof, the reader won't need a death defying act to practise this in life.

This book is a very personal memoir and the best means to appreciate it would be to take time to email the author. We would like to know how much you relate with the juddering journey of our protagonists.

www.ingramcontent.com/pod-product-compliance
Lightning Source LLC
LaVergne TN
LVHW091613170726
843492LV00007B/2393